The Murder Before Christmas

A Charlie Kingsley Mystery

The Murder Before Christmas

A Charlie Kingsley Mystery

by Michele Pariza Wacek

ISBN 978-1-945363-30-6

Library of Congress Control Number: 2021949748

For my family, for always believing in me.

Chapter 1

"So, Courtney, is it?" I asked with what I hoped was a comforting and nonthreatening smile. I set the mug holding my newest tea blend I'd created for the Christmas season—a variety of fresh mint and a couple of other secret ingredients—down on the kitchen table. I called it "Candy Cane Concoctions", and hoped others would find it as soothing as it was refreshing. "What can I do for you?"

Courtney didn't look at me as she reached for her tea. She was young, younger than me, and extremely pretty, despite looking like something the cat dragged in. (And believe me, I know all about what cats can drag in. Midnight, my black cat, had presented me with more than my share of gifts over the years.) Courtney's long, wavy blonde hair was pulled back in a haphazard ponytail, and there were puffy, black circles under her china-blue eyes. She was also visibly pregnant.

"Well, Mrs. Kingsley," she began, but I quickly interrupted her.

"It's Miss, but please, call me Charlie." Yes, she was younger than me, but for goodness sake, not THAT much younger. Maybe it was time to start getting more serious about my morning makeup routine.

Her lips quirked up in a tiny smile that didn't quite reach her eyes. "Charlie, then. I was hoping you could make me a love potion."

I quickly dropped my gaze, busying myself by pushing the plate of frosted Christmas sugar cookies I had made earlier toward her, not wanting her to see my shock and sorrow. She was pregnant and wanted a love potion. This just couldn't be good.

"I don't actually do love potions," I said. "I make custom-blended teas and tinctures."

Her eyebrows knit together in confusion. "But people have been raving about how much you've helped them. Mrs. Witmore swears you cured her thyroid problems."

I tried not to sigh. "My teas and tinctures do have health benefits, that's true. Certain herbs and flowers can help with common ailments. In fact, for much of human civilization, there were no prescription drugs, so all they had to use were herbs and flowers. But I can't promise any cures."

"What about Ruthie?" Courtney asked. "She claims those heart tinctures you made are the reason Bob finally noticed her."

I gritted my teeth. When Ruthie's dad was recovering from a heart attack, I made a couple of teas and tinctures for him. Ruthie, who had a crush on her coworker Bob for years, was apparently so desperate for him to notice her that one day, she decided to bring one of my tinctures to work (I'm unclear which) and slip it into his drink. And apparently, shortly after that, Bob started up a conversation with her, and eventually asked her out on a date.

It didn't help matters that Jean, Ruthie's mother, had claimed my tinctures had reignited her and her husband's love life, which is probably how Ruthie got the idea to try them with Bob in the first place.

Needless to say, that was an unintended benefit.

"I didn't give Ruthie a love potion," I said. "I gave her dad some tinctures and teas to help his heart."

Courtney gazed at me with those clear-blue eyes, reminding me of a broken-down, worn-out doll. "Well, isn't that where love starts?"

"Maybe," I said. "But my intention was to heal her father's heart, not to make anyone fall in love with anyone else."

"But it worked," she said. "Can you just sell me whatever you gave her? I have money. I'll pay."

"It's not that simple," I said. "I really need to ask you some questions. It's always good to talk to your doctor, as well."

She bit her lip and dropped her gaze to the tea in her hands. She looked so lost and alone, I felt sorry for her.

"Why don't you tell me a little bit about who you want this love potion for?" I asked. "That would help me figure out how best to help you."

She didn't immediately answer, instead keeping her eyes down. Just as I was starting to think she wasn't going to say anything at all, she spoke. "It's for my husband," she said, her voice so low, it was nearly a whisper.

I could feel my heart sink to the floor. This was even more heartbreaking than I had imagined. "You think your husband fell out of love with you?"

"I know he has," she said. "He's having an affair."

"Oh Courtney," I sighed. "I'm so sorry to hear that."

She managed a tiny nod and picked up her tea to take a sip.

"Have you two talked about it?"

She shook her head quickly.

"Does he know you know?"

She shrugged.

"Maybe that's the place to start," I said, keeping my voice gentle. "Having a conversation."

"It won't help," she said, her voice still quiet.

"How do you know if you haven't tried?"

She didn't answer ... just stared into her tea.

"Have you thought about marriage counseling?"

"He won't go." Her voice was firm.

"Have you asked?"

"I know. He's said before he thinks therapy is a waste of money."

"Okay. But you have a baby on the way," I said. "You need to be able to talk through things. I understand it might be diffi-cult to talk about something like *this*, but ..."

"He's in love with her." The words burst out of her as she raised her head. The expression on her face was so anguished that for a moment, it took my breath away.

"But how do you know if you haven't talked to him about it?"

"I just do," she said. "When you're married, you know these things. You can sense when your husband has fallen out of love with you. Hence, my need for a love potion. I need him to fall back in love with me. You can see how urgent this is." She gestured to her stomach. "In a few months, we're going to have a baby. I just *have* to get him to fall back in love with me."

Oh man, this was not going well. "I see why you would think that would be easier, but the problem is, there's no such thing as a love potion."

"Can you please just sell me what you made for Ruthie's dad? So I can at least try?"

"Whatever happened between Ruthie and Bob had nothing to do with one of my tinctures," I said flatly. "I don't want to give you false hope. I really think your best course of action is to have an open and honest conversation with him about the affair."

She was noticeably disappointed. It seemed to radiate out of every pore. I hated being the one to cause that, but I also wasn't going to sell her anything that could be misconstrued as a "love potion." Not only for her sake, but my own. The last thing I needed was lovesick women showing up at my door to buy something that didn't exist.

"Okay," she said quietly as she ducked her head so I couldn't quite see her face. "No love potion. How about the opposite?"

I looked at her in confusion. "The opposite?"

"Yes. Something that would kill him."

My mouth fell open. "Wha ... I'm sorry, could you repeat that?" I must have heard her wrong. She was still talking so quietly, not to mention hiding her face.

Courtney blinked and looked up at me. "I'm sorry?"

"I didn't hear what you said. Could you repeat it?"

"Oh. It was nothing." She offered an apologetic smile.

"No, really," I said. "I thought ..." I laughed a little self-consciously. "I thought you said you wanted something to kill your husband."

She blinked again. "Oh. Yeah. It was just a joke."

"A joke?"

"Yeah. I mean, you know. Sometimes married people want to kill each other. No big deal." Now it was her turn to let out a little twitter of laughter. "Have you ever been married?"

I shivered and put my hands around my mug to absorb the warmth. "No." Which was true. I had never been officially married, but that didn't mean my love life wasn't ... complicated.

Nor did it mean I didn't know exactly what she was talking about.

"Well, you know, sometimes married people can just get really angry with each other, and in the heat of the moment, even want to kill each other," she explained. "But they don't mean it. It's just because they love each other so much that sometimes that passion looks like something else. In the heat of the moment, in the middle of a fight, you can say all sorts of things you don't mean. But of course, they wouldn't *do* anything about it."

"Of course," I said. I decided not to mention that when she said it, she wasn't actually arguing with her husband. Nor did I bring up how perhaps she was protesting a bit too much.

I gave her a hard look as I sipped my tea.

She kept her gaze firmly on the table, refusing to meet my eyes. "Did I tell you how wonderful this blend is?" she asked. "It's so refreshing. Reminds me of a candy cane."

"Thanks. It's called 'Candy Cane Concoctions,' actually. I created it for the holidays," I said.

"It's wonderful." She took another hurried drink and put her mug down, tea sloshing over the side. "Are you selling it? Could I buy some?"

"Sure," I said, getting up from my chair. "Hang on a minute. I'll get you a bag."

She nodded as I left the kitchen to head upstairs to my office/work room. Although, to be fair, it was so small, it wasn't uncommon to find drying herbs or plants throughout the house.

I collected a bag and headed back to the kitchen. When I walked in, Courtney was standing up, fiddling with her purse. I instantly felt like something was off. Maybe it was the way she was standing or the bend of her neck, but she oozed guilt.

"Oh, there you are," she said, fishing out her wallet. "How much do I owe you?'

I told her, and she pulled out a wad of cash, handing me a twenty.

"I'll have to get you some change," I said.

"That's not necessary," she said, taking the bag. "You were so helpful to me, and besides, I need to get going."

"But this is way too much," I protested. "Just let me find my purse."

She waved me off as she left the kitchen and headed for the front door. "Nonsense. Truly, you were very helpful. No change is necessary." She jammed her arms into her coat, and without bothering to zip it up, opened the front door and headed out into the cold.

I closed the door after her, watching her through the window as she made her way down the driveway and into her car. She didn't seem very steady on her feet, and I wanted to make sure she got into her vehicle safely. After she drove off, I went back to the kitchen to look around.

Nothing appeared to be out of order. If she had been digging around looking for something (like something to kill her husband with), it wasn't obvious.

Still, I couldn't shake that uneasy feeling.

I went to the table to collect the dishes. Midnight strolled in as I was giving myself a pep talk.

"I'm sure she didn't mean it," I said to him. "She was probably just upset. I mean, she wasn't getting her love potion, and clearly, she was uncomfortable having a conversation with her husband. Although you'd think that would be a red flag."

Midnight sat down, his dark-green eyes studying me.

"Of course, that's hardly my business," I continued. "She's upset with him, and rightfully so. Who wouldn't be? Even if she wasn't actually joking in the moment, she was surely just letting off steam."

Midnight's tail twitched.

"Maybe this was even the first time she said it out loud," I said as I moved to the sink. "And now that she said it, she realized how awful it was. Of course she would never do anything like that." I turned to the cat. "Right?"

Midnight started cleaning himself.

"You're a lot of help," I muttered, turning back to the sink to finish the washing up.

As strange as that encounter was, it was likely the end of it.

I hoped.

Chapter 2

"Did you see the paper yet?"

"Good morning, Pat," I said into the phone. "So nice to hear from you. Oh, why yes, I did have a Merry Christmas. How was yours?"

"Go get your newspaper, and I'll be right over." There was a click, and the line went dead.

I replaced the receiver but didn't immediately move. There was a prickle of unease near the base of my skull. I had a sneaking suspicion I wasn't going to like what I saw in the newspaper.

Therefore, I took my time getting to it. I heated up water for a fresh pot of tea and put out some muffins I had baked the day before along with my new Christmas plates and napkins. Even though it was only me and Midnight, I still decorated the house—especially the kitchen. Normally full of sunflower decor, I had switched everything out for Christmas-themed items, complete with a small tree in the corner.

The whole Christmas season was bittersweet for me, but Christmas day was especially so. Christmas had always been my favorite holiday, but I missed seeing my niece Becca and my nephews, especially CB. My relationship with my sister Annabelle was still a little frosty. So, talking on the phone with them was easier.

After our call the day before, I'd spent a good chunk of the day baking before heading over to Nancy's house for Christmas dinner. Nancy, who owned the Redemption Inn, didn't have local family either, so we typically spent the holidays together at her place, where she could keep an eye on the inn.

The kitchen ready for Pat, I was about to fetch the paper when I decided I should maybe dress in something other than the old pair of grey sweatpants and sweatshirt I was wearing. I threw on a pair of jeans with one of my Christmas sweaters, red with a green tree in the center of it and ran a comb through my unruly brownish-blonde hair. It was somewhere between curly and frizzy, depending on the humidity, and today was definitely one of its wild days, so rather than deal with it, I pulled it back into a ponytail. I took a quick glance in the mirror, studying my eyes, which were an interesting mix of green, brown and gold, along with my full lips and narrow face, and wondered if I should dash on a bit of make up as well. I decided I didn't have enough time to mess around with it, and headed for the front door instead.

It was a cold, grey day outside. No snow yet, which was disappointing, as it would have been nice to have had a white Christmas. Still, it looked like it might start snowing any minute.

The paper was in the middle of the driveway, which meant I needed shoes. By the time I located my tennis shoes and laced them up, Pat had arrived and was heading up the driveway.

"Want to grab my newspaper while you're there?" I called out.

Her mouth dropped open. "You mean, you don't know yet?"

"It's Boxing Day, Pat," I said. "I didn't want to ruin Boxing Day."

"I don't even know what 'Boxing Day' means," Pat said as she detoured to scoop up my paper.

I shut the front door, knowing she would let herself in, and headed back to the kitchen to finish making the tea. I heard the front door open and close, and Pat appeared in the kitchen, her nose and cheeks bright red from the cold.

"I can't believe you didn't drop everything to get the paper," she grumbled, tossing it onto the table and snatching a muffin. Pat was a good decade or so older than me, and the best way to describe her was "round." She was plump, with a round face, round black-rimmed glasses, and short, no-nonsense brown hair that was turning grey. She had been one of my first customers, referred by Nancy, and had also become a good friend.

"Do you want to read it for yourself, or should I tell you?" she asked, taking a bite of the muffin. Like me, she also had on a Christmas sweater, except hers sported a family of snowmen holding song books and presumably caroling.

I brought the tea pot to the table and picked up the paper. "Neither," I said. "I told you, it's a holiday. Well, at least in Canada and the UK. We should be planning a shopping trip, not reading unpleasant happenings in the newspaper."

Pat rolled her eyes. "Trust me, you're going to want to see this," she said with her mouth full. "And, in case you didn't notice, we don't live in either Canada or the UK."

With a sigh, I slid the rubber band off and unrolled the paper.

A Murder Before Christmas, blared the newspaper. *Man Found Dead. Poisoned Present Suspected.*

"Poisoned *what*?" I muttered, reading the headline again. "Are they for real?"

"Don't worry about the headline," Pat said. "Just read the article."

I started to skim it.

Dennis Fallon, aged thirty-nine, was found dead in his home on Christmas Eve.

His wife, Courtney Fallon, aged twenty-five and six months pregnant, found him and called 9-1-1 ...

The words began to swim before my eyes. *Courtney Fallon ... six months pregnant.*

Had she told me her last name? I couldn't remember. But surely, this couldn't be the same woman.

An image of the haunted young woman who had sat in my kitchen a few weeks ago drinking my Candy Cane tea and asking for a potion to kill her husband appeared in my mind's eye.

It had to be someone else.

I quickly skimmed the article, searching for a photo of Dennis and his bride, when suddenly, my stomach twisted into a giant knot.

There, near the bottom. On their wedding day.

No question it was the same Courtney.

I looked up to see Pat pouring the tea. She handed me a mug. "You're going to need this. In fact, do you have anything stronger?"

I grasped the tea with limp fingers and collapsed into one of the chairs. "Pat, could I be responsible?"

Pat pulled out a chair and sat down across from me. "I don't know. Were you the one who sent him the poisoned brandy?"

"Poisoned bra ... *he was really poisoned*?"

"You didn't finish reading the article, did you?"

"No, I was just looking for a picture."

Pat shot me a look. "How many Courtneys do you think live in Redemption? Especially six-month pregnant ones?"

I picked up my tea to take a drink. It was hot and burned my tongue, but I drank it anyway. "I can't believe this is happening."

Pat reached for another muffin. "Oh, believe it. Do you want a muffin? Or should I find some Christmas cookies? I know you have some stashed in here somewhere ..."

Even though I had lost my appetite, I reached for a muffin. Maybe Pat had the right idea, and the sugar would help.

After Courtney left that day, I couldn't stop thinking about her. As much as I tried to write off what happened as frustration on her part—she didn't *really* want to kill her husband—I couldn't shake the feeling that something else was going on.

"Do you think I should tell someone?" I had asked Pat over tea and cookies.

Her expression was puzzled. "Who are you going to tell?"

"I don't know. The police?"

She blinked at me. "The police?"

"I mean, isn't that who you're supposed to tell if you have information about a crime?"

"Charlie, what exactly do you think you know? Someone came in here asking for a love potion because she's pregnant and her husband is cheating on her, and when it was clear she wasn't getting one, she asked for something else. You're talking about a pregnant woman who's upset because her husband is having an affair. There are probably a lot of women in that situation who have fantasized about killing their husband. Wouldn't YOU?"

I chewed on my lip. "I suppose."

What Pat had said made sense. The chances of her actually meaning it were pretty low.

And yet ...

Staring at Courtney's shy smile on the front page of the newspaper brought all my doubts back.

"So, do you want to tell me what happened, or do I need to read the article?"

Pat broke off a piece of muffin. "A package arrived for the mister on Christmas Eve. It appeared to be a present from one of his cousins, who just happened to be spending the holidays overseas. The note said something like 'Open me first for a little Christmas Eve cheer.' Inside was a bottle of his favorite brandy, so of course he had a little drink. Apparently, that's all it took."

"Where was Courtney when all this happened?"

"In the kitchen. She claimed they had decided to spend a quiet Christmas Eve at home, just the two of them, and she had spent the afternoon making a nice dinner. When he didn't show up, she went looking for him and found him lying on the floor of his study, dead."

My eyes widened. "Seriously?"

Pat nodded. "Yeah. Kind of weird, isn't it?"

"I'll say. Why would he be in his study drinking by himself when they were going to spend Christmas Eve together?"

"Good question."

"And she didn't hear him fall?" I continued. "You would think if a grown man collapsed, she would have heard it."

"Maybe she had Christmas music playing."

"Maybe." I frowned. "It still seems odd. So, after she found him, then what? Was she the one who called the cops?"

"Yep. And they pronounced him dead on the scene."

"This really does sound like she did it," I mused.

"Yeah, it does."

"Has she been arrested or charged or anything?"

"The paper didn't say," Pat said. "I would imagine they're keeping a close eye on her, though, at least."

"Maybe I should go talk to her," I said as I went back to studying Courtney's wedding photo. She looked impossibly young in a gorgeous wedding gown, her thick blonde hair piled on the top of her head. Her new husband was beaming at her.

"And say what? 'Hey, did you decide to poison your husband after all?'"

"Something like that, but maybe not quite as blunt." I couldn't tear my eyes away from her husband. Even if the news story hadn't mentioned his age, it was clear just in looking at him that he was much older than her, with his thinning hair and slight paunch.

But it was the look of love and adoration in his eyes that kept me glued to the page.

"I don't get it," I said.

"Get what?"

"Why he would cheat." I flipped the paper around to show Pat what I meant. "First of all, look at the age difference. She's young and pretty, and he's nearly middle age."

"So because he's middle aged, he wouldn't cheat?"

"No, but why would he? She appears to be a perfect trophy wife, if that's what he was looking for. But even more than that, look at how he's looking at her." I tapped the newspaper. "That doesn't look like a guy who doesn't love his wife."

Pat peered at the picture. "Maybe he fell out of love with her. We don't know when they got married."

"She's still pretty young. It couldn't have been that long ago."

"Maybe he's one of those guys who never wanted kids. And now that his wife is pregnant, he's lost interest."

"Possibly."

Pat glanced up at me, her eyes narrowing. "What are you saying? You don't think he was cheating on her?"

I thought about the visit with Courtney—how exhausted and depressed she had looked, and how sad she had been about her marriage. It sure didn't seem like she was acting; I had really felt her sincerity in thinking her husband was cheating on her.

"I'm not sure," I said. "I mean, Courtney sure seemed like she believed he was. But maybe she was wrong. Maybe he wasn't."

"How could she be wrong about something like that? How did she find out?"

"I don't know," I said. "I didn't ask. It didn't seem important at the time. But I do know they had never talked about it. So, it's possible she thought he was cheating for some reason, but he actually wasn't."

"Man, wouldn't it suck if she poisoned him over a misunderstanding?"

"What a nightmare." I sat back in my chair and stated twisting my ponytail around my hand. "I have to go see her. I mean, either he *was* cheating on her, which is unfortunate and kind of weird as she does seem to be a trophy wife, or he wasn't, but for some reason, she thought he was. Which is also weird."

"Or ..." Pat said, glancing at me out of the corner of her eye as she broke off another piece of muffin. "She made the whole cheating thing up."

I hadn't considered that theory. Was it possible she had invented the whole thing? I pictured her sitting at my kitchen table again, her beautiful blue eyes filled with sadness and grief. The idea she could have been faking caused a shiver to run up my spine.

I had to know the truth. Or at least, make an effort to find out what was going on. I ignored the little voice inside me that reminded me that this likely wasn't any of my business, and I had better things to do. I pushed myself out of my chair. "Want to come with me to visit the grieving widow?"

Pat tossed the last bite of muffin into her mouth. "Are you kidding? I wouldn't miss it for the world."

Chapter 3

Courtney's house was located on a quiet cul-de-sac on the other side of town near the lake. It was a large, two-story co-lonial home with red and white bricks, white trim, and a huge yard filled with trees and a massive garden. During the summer, it would probably be a real showstopper, but with dead grass, naked trees, and the garden a huge, dark gash in the middle of the yard, it looked barren and depressing.

Pat and I made our way up the driveway. The house was decorated with Christmas lights along with a plastic Santa in a sleigh and a family of snowmen, which was probably festive and fun at night, but in the middle of an overcast, grey day, it just added to the gloom.

I rang the doorbell and waited. The old wooden door was decorated with a cheery red and green wreath. I found myself wondering if all the holiday touches were Courtney's idea, and if so, if she would continue to do them next year. I hoped so, for the sake of her unborn child. He or she would probably have enough issues growing up without a father without losing Christmas, as well.

"Think she's not home?" Pat asked, stamping her feet and shoving her hands in her coat pockets.

"I guess we should have called first," I said, reaching over to ring the doorbell again.

The door burst open, causing me to jump. "Mrs. Kingsley! I mean Charlie. What are you doing here?"

Courtney looked awful. Her nose was bright red, and her face was puffy, like I had just interrupted her in the middle of a crying binge. Only part of her blonde hair was in a ponytail—the rest of it hung in a greasy, tangled mat around her shoulders. She wore a stained grey sweatshirt and sweatpants.

"I ... I'm so sorry for your loss," I said, feeling awkward and clumsy. I was ashamed that it hadn't occurred to me that I might be interrupting Courtney's grieving. I kept picturing her asking me for something to kill her husband with over and over, and I wondered if I had really seen the coldness in her eyes when she'd asked. "I wanted to come by and see if you needed anything, but I probably should have called first rather than barge in like this."

She sniffed loudly, rubbing her cheeks with a wet, crumpled tissue. "Do you want to come in?"

I glanced at Pat. "Well ... sure. If it's not too much trouble."

She shook her head. "The place is a bit of a mess, but if that doesn't bother you, come on in."

I stepped over the threshold, introducing her to Pat and handing her a basket filled with muffins. She sniffed again as she took it. "You didn't have to."

"It was no trouble," I said, wishing I had taken the time to make a casserole or something heartier than my leftover muffins.

She went to the kitchen while Pat and I moved toward the pristine living room. I wasn't entirely sure what she was talking about when she said the place was a mess. The only thing that seemed even a bit messy was the coffee table, which was covered with stacks of paperwork. The room was decorated in soft, pastel colors—yellows, pinks, and baby blues. The sofa and matching chairs were cream-colored with pillows and afghans matching the accent colors, and the hardwood floor was covered by a complementary braided rug. In the corner next to the fireplace was a huge Christmas tree with gaily wrapped presents beneath it.

"She's going to have to do a lot of baby proofing," Pat said, shaking her head as she sat down gingerly on the sofa.

Courtney came in at that point, saving me from answering. "Oh, where are my manners? Did you want anything? I could make a pot of coffee or tea. I still have some of that wonderful mixture I bought from you, or ..."

"We're fine, Courtney," I said gently. "Why don't you sit down?"

She looked a little lost, like she had her mind set on completing the task of making us something to drink, and now that she didn't have to, she wasn't sure what to do. But after a moment, she lowered herself into the chair.

"Are you doing okay?" I asked, feeling my face turn red in reaction to how stupid it sounded. "I mean," I started again. "The baby, and all."

"The baby is fine," she said, blowing her nose. "I'm doing about as well as can be expected, I guess. There's just so much to do, and I don't know where everything is. Dennis took care of all of that, but he's not here, so ..." Her face crumpled, and she scrubbed at it again with the tissue. "I'm so sorry. I'm emotional at the best of times, which these aren't. Thank you again for coming. That was so nice of you. Other than the cops and my mother, no one has stopped by."

I glanced at Pat, who raised her eyebrows at me. "No one has come by to offer their condolences?"

She shook her head. "It's probably because it's Christmas, you know. People are busy with their families and have other commitments. I'm sure they'll come once everything calms down in a few days."

"I'm sure that's all it is," I agreed, hoping she was right, and that it wasn't because everyone thought she had poisoned her husband. "Do you want to talk at all? About what happened?"

She blew her nose. "We were supposed to go to a party on Christmas Eve, but I wasn't feeling up to it. This whole month of December, it seemed all we did was go to one party after another. Not to mention all the gift-buying and decorating ... it was exhausting. Dennis had said we should take advantage of the fact that the baby wasn't here yet and do as much entertaining as possible, as next December, we would probably be homebodies. Initially, I agreed. It made a lot of sense. But, as December wore on, it just got more and more tiring. Christmas day was going to be a packed; we were seeing my mom for lunch and his family for dinner, and I just didn't think I could handle one more party. So, I asked if we could stay home and celebrate Christmas Eve with just the two of us. I would cook us a nice dinner, and we could light a fire in the fireplace and turn on the Christmas tree lights and have a nice, quiet evening.

"He agreed, so that afternoon I was busy in the kitchen cooking. I heard the doorbell ring, but I was in the middle of prepping the beef wellington, so I called out to Dennis to answer it. He came in to show me what Arthur had sent. It was beautifully wrapped ... gold paper with a red box. He said it was too pretty to unwrap, and maybe we should leave it, but he also couldn't resist seeing what it was, especially after he read the card. 'Open me first for some Christmas Eve cheer.' I think those words are burned in my brain." She sucked in a shaky breath. "Anyway, after Dennis read the card, he said something like, 'Leave it to Arthur to always know when to send a party in a box.'"

"Arthur is Dennis's cousin?" I asked.

She nodded. "He often sends things out of the blue, especially when he's traveling. He travels a lot."

"For work or ...?"

"Yes, for work, but for fun, too. I think he's in France now ... or maybe the Swiss Alps. It's hard to keep track of where he is most of the time." She paused, as if thinking about having a cousin who sent out-of-the-blue gifts and was difficult to get ahold of would be the perfect way to unsuspectedly slip someone some poison.

"What do you mean about the 'party in the box'?" Pat asked.

Courtney bit her lip. "Dennis wasn't happy about missing the Christmas Eve party," she said quietly. "He didn't say much about it, but I know he was disappointed. He was really looking forward to that one in particular. His client, Harry, was known for hosting really lavish parties. And, with the baby coming, this might be the last year in a long time we would be able to attend, at least the Christmas one. And ..." her voice trailed off before she gave herself a quick shake. "It doesn't matter now."

"What?"

She shook her head firmly. "No. It doesn't matter anymore. He was disappointed that we weren't going to the party. Period."

I glanced at Pat, seeing the same question in her eyes. What wasn't she telling us? "Was he upset with you about it?" I asked.

Her expression was puzzled. "Upset? No, not at all. He said he understood. He knew this holiday season was hard on me. It was just ... unfortunate. Bad timing. I should have mentioned something earlier, and we could have skipped some of the other parties instead of that one, and he was right ... I should have said something sooner."

"It's not your fault, you know," I said. I didn't particularly like how her wanting to stay home on Christmas Eve turned into her being at fault, but I also wasn't sure if I was simply reading too much into it. Her husband was dead, and maybe if they had gone to the party, he wouldn't be. It was natural for her to blame herself, even if it made no sense.

She gave me a watery smile that didn't quite reach her eyes. "I still should have said something sooner. Dennis was right. I should have trusted him to help me."

I thought about my initial conversation with Courtney, when she had first revealed that Dennis was cheating on her. She hadn't wanted to bring it up to him. Maybe this was more of a recurring theme. "Did you often not tell him things?"

She shrugged, staring down into her lap. "Sometimes. I don't know. His job was really stressful, and I didn't like adding to that."

"What did Dennis do for a living?"

"He's a financial advisor. He had his own business ... well, him and Glenn. That's his business partner."

Apparently, they were pretty successful at it, if the size of the house was any indication.

"What's going to happen to the business now?" Pat asked.

Courtney squeezed her tissue into a tighter ball. "I'm not sure. I guess Glenn takes it over completely."

Pat and I glanced at each other. I could see the same question mirrored in her eyes again. Is taking over a business a motive for murder?

"That does sound stressful," I said. "Managing other people's money."

"You have no idea," she said. "He had so much trouble leaving work at the office. Even though he has a home office, I felt like my role was to create a sanctuary for him here … a place for him to rest and recharge. He often told me how much he loved coming home, because it was just so soothing and peaceful after all the stress of the day. So, you can imagine how I didn't like to … disturb the peace, so to speak."

There was something there. I could feel it in the tension of the room. I wanted to keep asking questions to try and get to the bottom of whatever it was, but I didn't feel like it was the time or place. I wasn't sure if any of it was relevant to who killed Dennis, either.

I studied Courtney, who still had her head bowed. Every part of her screamed misery, from her collapsed shoulders to how her body seemed to want to curl into a tiny ball. Was asking her questions about her marriage really what I should be doing right now?

Probably not, I decided.

"So, back to the gift," I began. Courtney raised her head but didn't meet my eyes. I was feeling guilty pushing her with all my questions. No matter what happened in her marriage, she was way too young to be a widow. Especially since, in just a few months, she would also be a single mother. I needed to be more sensitive. "Dennis called it a 'party in a box' because he had to miss the Christmas Eve party?"

She nodded. "Yes, I think getting his favorite brandy … well, it felt like a sort of consolation prize or something. It really brightened his mood." She was silent for a moment, lost in the memories. I was expecting another bout of tears, but she remained dry-eyed.

"So, then what happened?" I prodded. "Did Dennis pour himself a drink?"

She shook her head. "No. Or at least, not in the kitchen. He told me he'd get out of my hair while I finished cooking. It was clear I wasn't really paying attention." She sucked in a shuddering breath. "Maybe I should have been more attentive. Then he might have stayed in the kitchen to have a drink with me instead of going off to his study. I could have seen when he collapsed and called the paramedics sooner. Maybe I could have saved his life."

"It's more likely that it wouldn't have mattered," I said. "Once we know what the poison was, we'll know more, but there's a number of them out there that either have no antidote, or they're so fast-acting, they might as well have no antidote."

Courtney didn't respond, instead reaching for a new tissue.

"So," I continued. "You don't know exactly when he had the brandy."

She shook her head. "I was so focused on making dinner, I wasn't really paying attention to the time. It wasn't until I had the stuffed mushrooms arranged on a plate that I realized I hadn't seen him for a while. That's when I found him in his study."

She pressed the clean tissue against her eyes for a moment. "He was slumped over, half on the sofa and half on the floor."

"Sofa?" I asked.

She nodded. "Along with his desk, he's got a black leather sofa in there. He likes, err liked, to sit and read on his sofa rather than at his desk. Especially right before dinner. That's how he unwound at the end of the day. He'd sit on the couch with a drink and a magazine or newspaper. He was forever reading financial publications." She paused again, took another shuddering sigh.

"As soon as I saw him, I ran over and touched him. I thought maybe he was having a heart attack or something. I shook him, and he collapsed the rest of the way onto the floor. It was at that point I knew he was dead."

That explained why Courtney didn't hear him fall. He must have been sitting on his sofa with his brandy when it happened.

"I called the paramedics," Courtney said. "At least, that's what I thought I was doing when I called 9-1-1. I was hoping they could revive him, but deep down, I knew it was too late. I still thought it was a heart attack or a stroke, even though he didn't have any medical issues … other than stress, of course. It didn't even occur to me he was poisoned. It was only when the cops arrived with the paramedics that I started to realize they thought something else was going on."

I glanced over to the hearth where the wedding photo that was in the newspaper was displayed. While it was clear Dennis was older than Courtney and that he had a few extra pounds on him, he didn't look like a candidate for a heart attack or a stroke.

Could she really be innocent? Despite asking about something to kill him with just a few weeks before?

"What did the cops say?" Pat asked.

Courtney balled her hands into fists. "They haven't said much yet, but it's clear they suspect me. They already came back to interview me again, although they pretended it was just to give me an 'update,'" she answered, adding air quotes around the word "update."

"What was the update? Do they know what killed Dennis?"

"Not yet. They're still waiting for the toxicology report. They're also testing the brandy and trying to get in touch with Arthur." She rolled her eyes. "Basically, they had absolutely nothing to report, but they certainly had a whole lot more questions for me. Why don't they do their job and investigate first, instead of harassing me?"

I forced myself to avoid looking at Pat. "Well, you do have to admit it looks suspicious," I said, trying to be gentle. "Your husband was poisoned at home, and you're the only witness."

"But it wasn't me!" she cried out. "I told them the brandy was a gift. I showed them the card. How could they think it was me?"

"Well," I said cautiously. "I'm guessing they might think you faked it."

Courtney's eyes went wide. "Faked it? How could I fake it? The gift arrived when I was in the kitchen."

I reminded myself that Courtney was grieving and not thinking straight. "The cops only have your word that the gift was delivered on Christmas Eve," I said. "Were you able to tell them who delivered it?"

"No, I told you. I was in the kitchen when the doorbell rang."

I nodded. "So what about Arthur? What kind of relationship did he have with Dennis?"

She gave me a perplexed look. "Arthur wouldn't have poisoned Dennis. That's ridiculous."

"But the gift came from Arthur ..."

"No, someone must have pretended," she said, like I was a particularly slow child. "If it did come from Arthur, it was clearly an accident. Arthur and Dennis got along great. Arthur would never have hurt Dennis on purpose."

"So you're saying someone sent the gift pretending to be Arthur, so Dennis wouldn't be suspicious about drinking it?"

"Yes. What else would it be?"

She still didn't seem to be grasping the situation she was in. "Okay, so let's look at this from the cops' point of view," I said. "You claim that this gift arrived on Christmas Eve for Dennis. You don't know how it arrived—you only heard the doorbell. Dennis tells you the brandy is from Arthur, who you're saying would never poison him. You're saying that there is someone out there who wanted to kill Dennis, and also knew him well enough to know he had a cousin named Arthur who is overseas right now. This person also knew you both would be home on Christmas Eve and not at this big party. And, you are the only witness to what happened that night."

Her face grew paler as I talked. "I'm in trouble, aren't I?" she asked faintly.

"It doesn't look good," I said. "You may want to call a lawyer."

She slumped over. "But it wasn't me. I swear. I'm telling the truth."

She was so distraught, I almost believed her. More than that, I *wanted* to believe her, but there were too many things that didn't add up. "Do they know about the affair?"

Courtney looked away. "I didn't tell them."

"Why not?"

"Because it doesn't matter anymore," she said. "Dennis is dead."

"Yes, but you must know they'll find out. If you don't say anything, it'll look even more suspicious."

Courtney chewed on her lip. "Well, they don't know I know."

She couldn't be this naive. It had to be an act. "What if they ask someone who knows you know?" I asked. "Like someone like me, who you told you wanted to kill Dennis ..."

Courtney jerked her head around, horror in her eyes. "I didn't mean it! I told you I didn't mean it!"

"I know," I said, trying to calm her down. "But what if you said something to someone else? Like Ruthie, when she told you about the love potion?"

Courtney was violently shaking her head. "I didn't tell anyone else. I swear. It just ... slipped out with you."

I found that difficult to believe. "Okay, okay. But how did the subject come up with Ruthie?"

Courtney rolled her eyes. "It was all her. She was telling everyone. I didn't have to ask."

If that was the case, I wondered how Bob would feel when he found out that Ruthie gave him a love potion. Although it was possible that he already knew and found it flattering she would go through such lengths for him.

"But," Courtney continued, her face brightening, "you could tell them."

I looked at her in confusion. "I could tell who, what?"

"The cops," she said, clapping her hands together. "You could tell the cops what I said."

My mouth dropped open. "You want me to tell the cops that you talked about killing your husband?" I couldn't be hearing her right.

"Yes," she said. "Charlie, don't you see? If I was really going to murder my husband, I wouldn't have told anyone about it. But the fact I talked about it with you proves I wasn't serious."

I eyed Pat, who looked as dumbstruck as I felt. "I don't think it works that way," I said cautiously. "I think the cops might consider that motive. Plus, I'll have to tell them that you knew about the affair, and then they'll think you definitely had motive."

Courtney's face crumpled. "I really messed things up, didn't I?" she asked softly.

"Maybe not," I said, even though I didn't believe it. "I'm not an attorney. I think you might want to call one."

She was shaking her head, her face anguished. "You gotta help me."

"I'm not really sure how I could," I said.

"Can you go talk to the cops?" she asked. "Maybe see if you can find out what they're thinking?"

"I don't think they're going to tell me that."

"But they have before," she said. "You've helped them with other cases. I remember hearing something about it. Maybe you could help them find who really killed Dennis."

Briefly, I closed my eyes. While it was true that I had worked with a couple cops previously—okay, one cop, Officer Brandon Wyle—it wasn't like we were friends or anything. More like they tolerated me.

Barely.

"I'm not sure my talking to the cops on your behalf would actually help you," I said. "I think a lawyer would be your best bet."

"But I don't have a lawyer right now," she said. "I have you. Will you please help?"

Those clear, china-blue eyes pleaded with me. Her chin quivered.

It was a bad idea. I knew it was. I should have listened to the little voice earlier, when I was home in my kitchen, that told me I should leave well enough alone. I really needed to just say, "No, I'm so sorry. This was a mistake." Then, if I still felt guilty, I could bring her a pan of my world-famous lasagna, so she at least wouldn't have to cook.

"Okay," I said instead. "I'll see what I can find out. But I don't want to have to lie about you knowing about the affair."

"You don't have to," she said quickly. "It's not like I lied to them. They asked if we had any problems in our marriage, and I said not any more than other couples. I mean, all couples have problems, right?"

"Yes, but ..." I started, but Courtney kept going.

"It's not like we fight or anything. We really don't. We've always gotten along so well." Her eyes filled with tears, and she blinked them back. "That's why I don't understand why he would do such a thing."

"Men are pigs," Pat said. "That's why."

I glanced back at the wedding photo again, at the look of love in Dennis's eyes. It didn't make sense to me either, but alas, it was too late to ask him now.

"The cops are still going to wonder why you didn't bring it up," I said.

"I'll just tell them I wasn't thinking straight. That I thought it was an accident, or the doctors made a mistake, and he had really died from a heart attack. I'll say I didn't think our private life was relevant."

I wasn't sure the cops would buy such a story, but if Courtney was as distraught with them as she had been with us, it was possible. Grief did make people do strange things.

"I'd feel better if you got yourself an attorney," I said. "An attorney might have a much better explanation."

"Okay, fine. I'll call and see if I can find one," she said. "But you're still going to go talk to the cops, right?"

"Yes," I sighed. "I'll see what I can find out. But no promises. Chances are, I will learn nothing helpful."

Courtney nodded her head vigorously. "Of course. And you'll tell them I didn't do it?"

"I'll do my best," I said.

Which I would, although I wasn't completely convinced of her innocence.

On one hand, it seemed like she had been completely blindsided by her husband's murder. And it also seemed like she truly loved him.

But, on the other, there was something off about her ... the way she was careful to avoid my gaze and hide her expression.

She was hiding something. I was sure of it.

The problem was, I had no idea what.

Chapter 4

"Tell me again—why are you here?" Officer Brandon Wyle shifted his lean, lanky figure into a more comfortable position as his chair squeaked in protest. His dark hair was longer than he normally wore it, curling around his collar and into curtain bangs that he absentmindedly brushed off his forehead. I found myself wondering if it was a new hairstyle, or if he kept forgetting to make an appointment with a stylist. His expression was carefully blank, but his dark eyes didn't miss a thing.

I was doing my best to sound more confident than I felt. The longer I sat there, the more convinced I was that it was a huge mistake. But at that point, it would have been even worse if I'd left, so I had to brazen my way through it. "She's my client," I said, which was true. She had bought some tea from me. Once. "And you've seen her condition."

Wyle's eyebrows went up. "'Condition'? You mean her pregnancy?"

"Exactly. Stress isn't good for mothers-to-be. Well, stress isn't good for any of us, but it's especially not good when you're pregnant. And she's already dealing with the stress of losing her husband ..."

"Who she likely poisoned," Wyle said.

Now it was my turn to raise eyebrows. "Are you saying she's a suspect?"

More squeaking as he moved again. We were sitting by his desk, which was tucked away in the corner of the police station. The room was too hot—Wyle had mentioned there was something wrong with the heater—but the combination of the heat, cigarette smoke, and the burnt-coffee-old-sweat odor made my stomach turn. Even though we weren't alone, no one appeared to be paying any attention to us. The constant collective noise of the phone ringing, typewriters clacking, and people talking filled the space. "Oh come on, Charlie. You're smarter than this. Everyone is a suspect in the beginning. Heck, you even made the list."

I was aghast. "Me?"

"Yes, you. Don't you think it's pretty suspicious you're even here?"

"I never even met Dennis," I said.

"You don't need to meet the guy to sell his wife some poison."

"I don't sell poison," I said firmly, deciding I would definitely not be mentioning Courtney's request for something to kill her husband to Wyle. "I sell teas and tinctures."

"Uh huh." Wyle tapped his pen on his notebook, which was balanced precariously on top of a stack of paperwork. His eyes continued to study me.

Wyle was not my first choice. I'd have preferred a cop who didn't know me from Adam. Preferably someone who would be open to my flirtations and maybe let slip a tidbit or two, so I would have something to tell Courtney. And Pat.

Even better, one who wouldn't think to tell anyone I had come by asking questions.

Instead, I got my last choice. Well, maybe my second-to-last. Officer Murphy might be a better last choice. He was sure I had something to do with a couple of disappearances a few years before, but could never prove anything, which meant he continued to regard me with great suspicion … even when it was clear I had nothing to do with the case at hand.

Tough call.

But, seeing as I was stuck with Wyle for the moment, I was going to have to make do. "Look," I said. "Don't you think it's too obvious to be Courtney? I mean, if you were going to kill your husband, why on Earth would you do it when it was just the two of you alone in the house? You're just asking for 'number one suspect' status."

"You're assuming criminals are smarter than they are," Wyle said.

"Have you spoken to her? She's grieving pretty heavily."

"Could also be a guilty conscience."

"Wyle, come on," I said. "Would it be possible to investigate a few other people before throwing the book at her?"

Wyle started jotting down a note. "Who would you like to start with? You, perhaps?"

I ignored that. "Have you talked to Arthur?"

"It's not him."

"How can you be so sure?"

Wyle sighed. "Well, first of all, the package wasn't mailed. It was delivered by courier. And, before you ask, yes, we were able to track down Arthur, and it seemed pretty clear he didn't know anything about it."

While I figured Arthur was a long shot based on Courtney's reaction, it was still a little deflating to hear he had been ruled out. "Did you ask the courier who sent it?"

Wyle's eyes went wide. "Oh, what a good idea. You should be a detective."

I gave him a look. "I guess that means the courier was a dead end."

"You guessed right. The package was mailed to the courier with instructions to deliver it on Christmas Eve."

"Who mailed it?"

"It arrived a few days ago, so all the mailing material had been thrown away. And before you ask, the person paid with cash and left delivery instructions. I guess this isn't that strange— people mail or drop packages off with special delivery instructions."

Wyle was right; that wasn't very helpful. "What about his business partner?"

Wyle shrugged. "What about him?"

The fluorescent lights flickered. I wasn't sure what was worse: the lights, the heat, or the smell. Regardless, it—or maybe the combination—was starting to give me a headache. "Well, don't you think it's at least worth having a conversation with him?"

"Why? Is there something suspicious about him or the business?"

"No, not that I know of," I said. "But that doesn't mean there isn't something TO know."

Wyle gave me a look and wrote something down with an exaggerated flourish. "Talk to business partner, check. Anyone else?"

My headache was getting worse. I started rubbing my temple, trying to ease the pain. I really ought to bring up the affair. The sooner I did that, the sooner I could get out of the whole ordeal. But they were already so suspicious of Courtney ... wouldn't that make it worse?

Wyle's eyes narrowed. "Charlie? What is it?"

I sighed. If they didn't know about it now, they were going to find out at some point, and maybe I could try and mitigate some of the damage. "Dennis was having an affair."

Wyle's expression didn't change, but something seemed to shift in it—like he was suddenly hyper-focused. "Do you know with who?"

I shook my head.

"Does Courtney know?"

I looked away. I didn't want to answer as I felt like all I was doing was driving more nails in Courtney's coffin. "She thought Dennis was having a heart attack," I said.

"He's thirty-nine. Pretty young for a heart attack."

"Yes, but he's quite a bit older than she is," I said. "And remember, she's pregnant and not thinking straight."

Wyle gave me a look.

"For the record, I told her she should have told you," I said. "She said she didn't because she didn't think it mattered anymore. He's dead."

"But we told her we thought he was poisoned," Wyle said.

"She didn't believe you," I said. "She thought there had been some sort of mistake, or that it was an accident."

Wyle didn't look convinced.

"Everyone grieves differently," I said. "And yes, I get that it sounds suspicious, but she's really not thinking straight."

"I'll make a note," he said drily. "How long has the affair been going on?"

"I don't know the details, but it's been a while," I said.

He nodded and wrote a few things down. "Is that it?"

I paused, trying to figure out if I'd made things worse for Courtney. I had an unpleasant feeling the answer was "yes." Was there anything I could do to make it better?

No. I'd better stop while I was ahead.

"Yes, that's it." I stood up. Wyle stood as well.

"Thanks for coming in," he said. "I'll definitely look into all this."

"Of course," I said, picking up my purse.

Wyle didn't move. "Which means you don't need to do anything more."

"What more do you think I would do?"

Wyle huffed a sigh. "No investigating. We'll take it from here."

I gave him a thin smile. "I don't know what you're talking about. I don't investigate anything. I make teas." I turned and headed toward the door.

"I'm serious, Charlie," Wyle called out.

I waved at him without turning around. I couldn't get out of there fast enough.

***

"Well, that was pretty unproductive," Pat said, picking up a fry. "Unless you count getting yourself added to the suspect list. Then, it was definitely a win."

I made a face at her.

We were sitting in Aunt May's Diner. After leaving Courtney's house, Pat assumed she would be accompanying me to the police station. I assumed I was dropping her off at her house. While in the car, we'd had a brief (but heated) discussion about it. I argued that me showing up at the station was odd enough as it was, let alone arriving with a second person, which would surely raise even more red flags. In the end, we came to a compromise. Pat agreed, a little less graciously than I thought warranted, to not try and weasel her way into the station with me. I agreed to meet her at Aunt May's afterward to give her the lowdown.

"And you better not leave anything out," she warned as she slammed the car door. I gave her a cheery smile as I pulled away from the curb. She stood in front of Aunt May's, watching me drive away and shaking her head.

"We for sure now know Courtney is a suspect," I said, playing with the straw in my ginger ale. My stomach was still queasy, although as soon as I got out of the station, I started feeling much better. I decided on the grilled cheese with tomato soup, which was also helping. "And the cops don't seem to be looking at anyone else."

"Wyle did say lots of people were on the suspect list," Pat said, wiping her hands with a napkin. She had ordered a club sandwich and eaten most of it while waiting for me. "It's possible they haven't settled on Courtney yet."

"True," I said, frowning darkly at my own sandwich as I pictured Wyle's smug smile while making a point of taking notes. Oof, that man drove me crazy. "But it feels like they've decided it's Courtney, and all that's left is for them to cross all their T's and dot their I's."

"It's hard to blame them," Pat said. "It does look suspicious."

I eyed her. "You think she's guilty, too?"

Pat shrugged. "You were there with me. She's hiding something."

"Yeah," I said glumly, going back to staring at my sandwich. "I wish I knew what that was."

Pat regarded me thoughtfully. "Why does it bother you so much to think she might have killed her husband? I mean, you barely know her. She wasn't a client. Buying one bag of tea doesn't count, so it's not like you're going to lose business."

"It doesn't bother you?"

Pat shrugged. "Sure, it's a little creepy to think we were sitting in a murderer's living room, but he *was* cheating on her. It's not like we were in danger."

"But was he?" In my mind's eye, I saw the wedding photo again.

Pat pursued her lips. "People fall out of love, Charlie," she said, as though reading my mind.

"I know."

"And just because someone is unfaithful, it doesn't mean he doesn't love his spouse."

"I get it," I said impatiently. "But that doesn't change the fact that there's just something about this that doesn't add up." I paused and started playing with my straw again. "I can't put my finger on it."

"Maybe it's because you've never chit chatted with a murderess before."

I jerked the straw so hard, ginger ale sloshed out of the glass.

"Or," Pat continued, not noticing the mess I'd made, "maybe Courtney is being set up."

I gave Pat a hard look. "Weren't you just trying to convince me that Courtney is guilty?"

Pat grinned at me. "I didn't say I believed it. I was just throwing it out there as a reason for your uncomfortable feeling." Her smile disappeared. "But seriously. I agree with you. There's something not quite right about all of this. But what?"

But what, indeed. Was it because Courtney was being set up for her husband's murder? Or was she responsible?

Or was something else going on completely?

I picked up my sandwich. "I suspect we'll never know the truth."

Pat huffed a dramatic sigh. "And that's probably the truest statement we've heard today."

Chapter 5

I was in the middle of creating a customized tea blend for one of my clients when the doorbell rang. Hoping it wasn't her yet, as I was running behind, I hurried to the door.

However, the woman standing on the other side of the door was a stranger.

"Can I help you?"

She was older, her face soft with wrinkles. Her blonde hair streaked with silver was pulled back in a stylish bun, and her clear, blue eyes studied me from behind silver, cat-eyed frames. She wore a long, cream-colored wool coat and a bright-red scarf around her neck. She seemed familiar, but I couldn't place her.

"Are you Charlie Kingsley?" she asked.

"I am. And you are ..."

"Violet. Violet Simson." She held out her hand. "I'm Courtney's mother."

Of course. The resemblance was striking; I couldn't believe I hadn't seen it sooner. I reached out my hand to shake hers, but then I realized I was letting all the heat out of the house, so I stepped back to invite her in. She took a moment to stomp her feet on the doormat before coming inside.

"Do you want some tea?" I asked, shutting the door behind her.

Her face brightened. "Do you still have some of the candy cane kind?"

"Sure do." I headed to the kitchen to get a pot started. "Just hang your coat on the rack and come join me."

She appeared in the kitchen a few moments later, wearing a bright-blue sweater that matched her eyes and black slacks. "Your kitchen is so big," she exclaimed.

I glanced around, taking in the white cabinets, grey counter-tops, and huge island in the center. I still had my Christmas decorations up, including the tree in the corner and a Santa cookie jar. "Yes, it certainly is."

"I miss my big kitchen," she said with a sigh. "My apartment is nice, but I sure miss my kitchen. And wow! Your garden!" Violet had moved to the large window and was longingly staring out.

"Not much to look at now, I'm afraid," I said as I carried the tea and a couple of mugs to the table.

She waved a hand dismissively. "I can get a good idea of what you're doing. My garden is something else I miss." She sighed again.

"I'd miss my garden and kitchen too," I said as I deposited the last of my leftover Christmas cookies in the center of the table next to the pot. They were nearly a week old, but they still tasted fine. Hopefully, Violet would finish them, or maybe I could persuade her to take the rest with her, as I was Christmas-cookied out. I poured the tea as she took a seat. Immediately, she cupped the mug with her hands, but she didn't drink.

"How is Courtney?" I asked, figuring the question would eventually lead to why she had turned up on my doorstep.

She let out a deep, painful sigh. "That's why I'm here today."

I pushed the Christmas cookies a little closer to her. A little sugar and fat certainly couldn't hurt. "I thought that might be the case."

She smiled, but it appeared strained, and her eyes remained worried. "I knew you'd understand. I had a feeling you were the right person to talk to."

I could feel prickles of unease start to rise on the back of my neck, but I kept my expression neutral. "Oh?"

She nodded. "Courtney needs help."

I had no doubt Courtney needed help. Probably a lot of it. "Has she hired a lawyer yet?"

Violet sighed again and looked up at the ceiling. "She's called a few people, but everyone thinks she's guilty."

I restrained from saying the obvious—that a lot of people thought Courtney was guilty because she looked pretty guilty—hence, her need for an attorney. The sooner the better. "Is that what they said?"

"Not in so many words."

"Are they refusing to work with her?"

"No, they're all willing to represent her."

"Then what's the problem?" I didn't understand what Violet was upset about, nor what she thought I could do to help. Was she looking for suggestions?

"She has no one on her side," Violet burst out, sloshing her tea over the side of her mug and onto her hand. She quickly jerked her hand away and thrust one of her fingers into her mouth.

"Did you burn yourself?" I asked, getting out of my seat. "Let me get you a washcloth."

"It's nothing," she mumbled around her fingers, but I was already at the sink, wringing out a washcloth for the table and a clean one for her hand. I handed her one and wiped up the table with the other.

"Okay," I said, sitting back down. "Let's back up here. First off, how can you be so sure no one is on her side?"

"Isn't it obvious?" Violet asked, finally succumbing to the lure of the sugar and reaching for a cookie. "No one is coming by. No one. Not to bring food, not to see how she's doing. They're not even sending flowers."

"Well, it's tough to know what to say or do in these situations," I said. "Her husband has been murdered. It's not like he died of cancer or a car accident."

"And they think she did it."

"Well, some probably do," I agreed. "But some probably don't know what to think."

Violet took a bite of the cookie, spilling crumbs over the table. I made a mental note to bring small plates to the table with snacks. Seeing Violet at the door had thrown me off my game. "If they were real friends, they would come by," Violet said darkly, brushing a few crumbs off her chin. "These cookies are very good, by the way," she added. Before I could respond, she kept talking. "But it's more than just her so-called 'friends,'" she said around another bite of cookie. "The cops think she's guilty, too."

'The cops think everyone is guilty," I said. "It's their job."

"Yes, but if they're already convinced Courtney is guilty, they're not going to look at anyone else."

This was true, and it was something that had bothered me, as well. But, somehow, coming from Courtney's mother, it simply ratcheted up my uneasy feeling.

"That's why I thought Courtney should get herself a good attorney," I said.

Violet pressed her lips together into a straight line. A couple of crumbs were stuck to the corner of her pink-lipsticked mouth. "If the attorney thinks she's guilty, too, he isn't going to try and find the real killer, either," she said. "Courtney needs someone in her corner. Someone who will fight for her."

Oh no. I had a terrible feeling where she was going. "Have you thought about hiring a private investigator?" I asked. "I mean, if you think the cops aren't going to look hard enough, a PI could help."

She waved her hand in a dismissive way. "A PI is going to be just like an attorney. He'd take her money, sure, but he'll assume she's guilty and not try all that hard."

"I don't think it works that way ..." I started to say, but Violet interrupted me.

"That's why she needs you." She looked me directly in the eyes. "She needs you to help investigate and find the real killer."

My stomach twisted in a knot. I thought about Wyle a few days before, his dark eyes boring into mine as he told me to leave the investigation alone. What would he do if he knew the mother of his number one suspect was in my house trying to get me to do exactly what he warned me against doing? "You do know I'm not a detective or anything," I said. "I make teas and tinctures."

"But you have done some investigating before," she said. "Right?"

42

"Yes, but ..."

"And you believe she's innocent, right?"

I wouldn't say that, exactly. But her eyes, so like her daughter's, were so hopeful, I couldn't bear to crush her spirits. "Believing in her guilt or innocence doesn't have anything to do with finding the person who is responsible."

"But you'll try harder if you believe in her innocence," Violet insisted. "We can pay you, if that's what you're worried about."

"No, that's not it." My tea business did pretty well, better than I ever thought it would, and my trust fund covered the mortgage payment, so money wasn't an issue. I took a deep breath. "I'm just a regular person," I said. "I don't have any special skills or a license or anything. I don't know if my poking around is going to help Courtney or make things worse." Thinking about my previous conversation with Wyle, I was leaning toward it making things worse.

"But that's not true," Violet said. "Courtney told me you already talked to the cops on her behalf."

"Yes, but I don't know how helpful I was." I had called Courtney to give her an update, which I didn't think was terribly optimistic. I told her the cops now knew about the affair, but that I had also pushed them to question other people, including Dennis's business partner. I didn't mention that I didn't think I was terribly successful at the latter, although in retrospect, I probably should have. Both mother and daughter now appeared to think I had made a difference in the case, hence their desire for me to keep investigating for them.

"The point is, you're trying to be helpful," Violet said firmly. "And that's what we need. Will you help us?"

I looked into Violet's clear, china-blue eyes, so like her daughter's, and inwardly sighed. How did I get myself into these messes?

"I'll see what I can do," I said, and Violet clapped her hands.

"I knew you were the perfect person! I just knew it."

I smiled back, but it felt forced and uncomfortable. Hopefully, I would accomplish more than just turning myself into more of a suspect.

* * *

"Do you even know the first thing about investigating a crime?" Pat asked.

We were sitting in the living room with the lights off and the Christmas tree on. I figured since it wasn't yet New Year's, we could still enjoy the Christmas tree without guilt. I had also poured us both a healthy glass of red wine. I wasn't much of a drinker, maybe one or two glasses a month, but it felt warranted.

"I've done it before," I said.

Pat raised her eyebrows over the rim of her wine glass. "You got lucky before," she corrected. "This is a little different."

"How so?"

"Well, to start, do you know where to begin?"

"Violet gave me the names of Dennis's business partner and, uh, mistress."

Pat's eyes went wide. "Mistress? So Courtney knows who she is?"

I took a sip. "Apparently so."

"Did Violet tell you how Courtney found out?"

"I didn't ask. Trust me, it was weird enough getting that information from Courtney's mom." I could still remember the face Violet made as she wrote down the woman's name, address, and phone number.

"I'm just ... I can't believe Courtney didn't say something to Dennis about it before. If I had found out the name of some floozy Richard was cheating on me with, you can bet your bottom dollar we would have had a chat about it."

"I don't understand it either," I said.

"So, is that it?"

"For now," I said. "I also got some background information on Dennis. As it turns out, he was married before, to a woman named Nina."

Pat rolled her eyes. "Let me guess. Divorced."

"You win the prize."

Pat shook her head. "So, Courtney really was a trophy wife. Did he leave Nina for her?"

"That I don't know, and I could hardly ask her mother."

Pat inclined her head. "Fair enough. Are you going to have a chat with Nina?"

"I'm strongly considering it. An ex-wife would certainly have motive to not just murder her 'husband,' but set his new wife up for the crime. The timing doesn't make a lot of sense, though. Courtney and Dennis have been married a couple of years now. I would have thought if Nina was inclined to do such a thing, she would have done it before now. Especially as Courtney has a baby coming."

"Maybe the baby is what pushed her over the edge," Pat said. "Maybe Nina wanted a baby, and Dennis kept refusing, and then she found out the new wife is pregnant."

"Hmm, good point," I said, drumming my fingers on my wine glass. "I think I definitely need to pay her a visit."

"Anyone else on your list?"

"Not yet. I asked Violet to think about any other people who would have known about Arthur and would want to hurt Dennis."

"What about Dennis's family?"

"I asked, but Violet doesn't really know them very well. She was going to get a list together for me with some notes. But clearly, she wanted me to start with Glenn and, uh, Tiffany."

Pat's jaw dropped. "Tiffany? Really? That's his mistress's name?"

"It gets worse."

"Worse?"

"She's an aerobics instructor."

Pat choked on her wine. "Wow. I feel like I'm living in a bad soap opera. Tiffany the aerobics instructor! I can practically picture what she looks like." She wagged her eyebrows at me, and I snorted.

"But seriously," Pat continued. "I'm glad you got the names, but how on Earth are you going to approach either of them?

You're not the cops. You can't just sashay in and start asking questions about Dennis."

"Let's just say I have a few tricks up my sleeve," I answered mysteriously.

Chapter 6

"Get those knees up," Tiffany shouted from the front of the room. "You don't want those Christmas cookies stuck on your thighs."

I groaned. At this point, I didn't care if every Christmas cookie I had ever eaten decided to move into my thighs. They could even bring their friends.

"And smile!" Tiffany demonstrated by pointing at her own wide grin.

I groaned again.

Back when I lived in New York, I regularly attended aerobics classes. Moving to Redemption, I had been so busy with gardening and tea-making, not to mention cleaning my huge old house, that I never seemed to have the time to go to aerobics. But when I called the Fit for Life health and fitness club for Tiffany's teaching schedule, I figured it wouldn't be a big deal. I mean, I was a little out of shape, but I was sure the class was nothing I couldn't handle.

I thought I was going to die.

Tiffany, in contrast, didn't even look like she had broken a sweat. Her platinum-blonde hair was pulled back in a high ponytail that bounced merrily along with the music, and her hot-pink and green leggings with matching pink leotard seemed to glow under the fluorescent lights. Her body was tight and firm, including her derrière, which I caught frequent glimpses of in the wall-to-wall mirror. My own reflection wasn't nearly as flattering.

All in all, Tiffany looked exactly like one would imagine an aerobics instructor named "Tiffany" who was having an affair with a married man would. I knew without any doubt that Pat would be rolling her eyes if she were there. Of course, she would never be in such a class with me, because Pat was also much smarter than me.

This was definitely not one of my best ideas.

It got even worse. Tiffany put us through a torturous routine of leg lifts and sit-ups before guiding us through a few stretches to end class.

I mopped off my face with a towel and uncapped my water bottle for a drink, trying to pull myself together enough to have a conversation with Tiffany. Although I was wondering if I should figure out another way to run into her going forward—something that didn't involve me doing aerobics.

"Nice to see a new face in class."

Startled, I nearly choked on my water. There she was, standing right next to me. Now that I was closer, I could see she was both older and sweatier than I had thought. Tiny lines fanned out from a pair of intense green eyes, and beads of sweat dotted her forehead and cheeks, almost puddling on top of her heavy makeup.

"Thanks," I said. "It's been a little while since I've been to a class. I'll definitely be feeling it tomorrow."

She grinned. "I'll take that as a compliment. I don't remember seeing you around. Are you new?"

"Sort of. I moved to Redemption from New York a few years ago. When I lived in New York, I was pretty religious about attending aerobics class, so I thought maybe it was time to get back into the groove."

"Well, you're starting at the right time," she said. "We have a special going on, a New Year, New You type of thing. Half off monthly membership dues for six months."

"That's a great deal and probably exactly what I need," I said as I fell into step next to her.

"I can get you signed up if you want," she said and laughed. "Sorry, not trying to be pushy. But I also know human nature. If you don't plunk down a payment, you're far less likely to come back."

"Ain't that the truth?" I said. "I'm just not used to an aerobics teacher selling me memberships."

"Oh, I'm more than an instructor," she said. "I own the place."

My eyes widened. Violet hadn't mentioned that. "Oh, wow. I didn't realize."

"Yeah, it's all mine." She waved her arm in a big flourish, the gesture encompassing the locker rooms, weight room, cardio room, and aerobics studio. "It's probably not as impressive as what you're used to in New York, but it does the job."

"I think it's lovely." Which was true. While it wasn't as shiny and polished as the clubs in New York, it was clean and bright, with pale-yellow walls, hardwood floors, and colorful inspirational posters all around. The one in the hallway had a kitten dangling from a rope, with the words "Hang In There" printed across the bottom. The location wasn't bad, either. It was a couple of blocks away from downtown, and it had a nice, big parking lot in front.

Her face flushed with pleasure. "Thanks. You should have seen it before the remodel. It was a wreck." Her hands fluttered around, as if giving me a tour of what it once looked like. "I'm Tiffany, by the way. Tiffany Gold."

"Charlie Kingsley." We shook hands. Her nails were long and polished in a bright, cheery red, probably in celebration of Christmas.

"So, Charlie, think I'll be seeing you again?"

I smiled. "Probably." *Most definitely.* I suspected I would need at least one or two more visits before I was able to start asking her about Dennis and Courtney.

Her smile was wide. "Great. Let me get you the paperwork. You can take it home, of course, or we can fill it out here."

"That works," I said as I followed her to the cozy lobby filled with comfortable chairs and small tables. The color scheme was muted and soothing—browns, beiges, and blues, and there were more framed inspirational posters featuring cats, like the one with a cat balancing on a branch and the words "Believe in yourself, and you can do anything." The Christmas decorations were still up, including a tree covered with red and gold tinsel. On the opposite wall from it was a bar with a couple of poinsettias on it. Three high chairs stood in front of what looked like a place for meal preparation, but other than a tall fridge filled with water and energy drinks, it was bare.

"What do you do, Charlie?" Tiffany asked as she headed for the desk that stood next to the front door. There had been someone manning it when I walked in—a tiny, perky thing who didn't look old enough to drive—but the room was empty now. I saw Tiffany shake her head slightly as she walked over to the desk.

"I sell teas and tinctures," I said.

She paused and glanced over her shoulder to look at me. "What kind of teas?"

"My own custom blends mostly. The tinctures are custom, too."

She turned all the way around. "Really? Where do you get the ingredients?"

"Grow them. Mostly. Not all, of course. It's a little too cold for a lemon tree, for instance. But I grow many of the flowers and herbs myself."

"Are they organic?"

"Yep."

She clapped her hands together. "This is amazing! I've been looking for someone like you!"

"Really?" I hadn't expected that. "Do you have something going on that you think an herbal tea would help with?"

"Maybe. I've been using herbs and teas for years. But the distributors are all out of town, so they have to mail me products and mixtures. Which is fine, but it won't work with the idea I had."

"Which is ..."

"Doing something here."

"Here?"

She nodded toward the long counter. "I've been wanting to offer some healthy beverages, and maybe some snacks, so people can sit after their workout and have something. I could offer coffee, but ..." she made a face. "I don't know. Coffee doesn't feel like it belongs. It's got all that caffeine, and I don't know if people should be drinking caffeine after a workout when they should be rehydrating. But herbal tea, that's perfect."

"Maybe I could come up with a post-workout blend," I said, the wheels already turning.

Her eyes widened. "You could do that?"

"Yeah, something to help relax the body and reduce inflammation. Maybe rose and chamomile. Ginger would be good, as well. I can play around, maybe come up with a couple of versions."

She let out a little squeal. "Oh! I love that idea. Yes, a custom tea blend. Maybe we can make it exclusive to Fit for Life."

"Maybe." I hadn't thought about doing custom tea blends for another business, but the idea intrigued me.

Tiffany was so excited, she looked like she might break out into another aerobics routine. "This is so perfect. It's exactly what I hoped would happen."

Hoped would happen? I shot her a funny look. "What do you mean?"

She gave her head a quick shake. "Nothing. Well, almost nothing. It's just I never wanted this to be solely a health and fitness club. I always wanted it to be more holistic. You know, offer healthy foods, maybe teach classes on nutrition and stress reduction, like meditation and yoga. You know, everything that goes into being fit for life." Her smile was a little self-conscious. "But it's been a more difficult road than I thought to add those other pieces. Just running the fitness part has taken up most of my time."

"Is there anyone who can help out? Maybe a family member or husband?" I tamped down my eagerness, not wanting to scare her off. Maybe I would be able to get more out of her today than I had hoped.

She let out a bitter laugh. "No, my family doesn't live that close, not that any of them would be interested. And my husband considers this my hobby." She rolled her eyes.

I tried not to let my shock show.

She had a husband.

I had assumed she was single.

"He thinks this is a hobby?"

She nodded. "He makes enough that I don't need to work, but I was getting so bored with volunteer work, and this was what I always wanted to do. So, he did give me the money to get it going, and I'm grateful, but ..." her voice trailed off, and she looked away. I could see a muscle tightening in her jaw. "Oh my goodness, look at the time! I have another class coming up. Do you want to come back later, maybe in a couple of days, and we can hammer out the details to sell your tea?"

"Sure." I was dying to ask more questions, especially about this non-supportive husband, but the brittle smile she had plastered on her face made it clear she was done talking about it. At least for now.

"Jillian," she called out, and the petite teenager I'd seen earlier appeared from the hallway. "Can you help Charlie here? She's going to be a new member. And schedule a time for us to meet in a couple of days."

"Sure," Jillian answered in a sing-song voice as she headed to the desk.

Tiffany's smile turned frosty. "And please remember what I told you about not leaving the front desk unattended."

Jillian bobbed her head, her ponytail bouncing up and down. "Yes, Ms. G."

"Thanks," Tiffany said shortly before turning to me with a slight nod. "See you soon."

"Can't wait." Which was absolutely true. There was clearly more going on than what "met the eye," and I was impatient to discover what was lying beneath the surface.

Chapter 7

"So, Mrs. Kingsley, why don't you tell me a little bit about yourself?" Glenn smoothed his red tie as he seated himself behind the imposing oak executive desk in front of me. Like Dennis, he appeared to be in his late thirties or early forties, with a receding hairline and the beginnings of a round, soft belly. A mustache covered what appeared to be a pair of thin lips, and his cheeks and nose were ruddy, as if he'd enjoyed a little too much alcohol over the years. He adjusted his well-cut navy suit jacket and selected a pen from a holder.

"It's 'Ms.,'" I said, trying to unobtrusively make myself more comfortable on the hard-backed chair in front of him. "I'm not married."

He made a note on the empty notepad in front of him. "Widowed or divorced?"

"Neither," I said.

The faintest hint of surprise crossed his face, so quickly I thought I might have imagined it. But I was pretty sure I hadn't. He made a second note. "So how can I help?"

There was a fussiness about him that I found off-putting. Something about the meticulously clean desk, save for the notepad, a black and gold blotter, a matching black and gold pen holder, a letter tray (empty, of course), a gold-framed picture angled so I couldn't see who was in it, and a mug with the words "World's Best Boss" printed across it set my teeth on edge. There was no sign of any Christmas decorations, although to be fair, it was after the new year. And last but not least, the uncomfortable chairs. I was starting to wonder if Glenn chose them specifically because of how uncomfortable they were—a subtle hint to not linger or waste any time with friendly banter.

Even though I had never met Dennis and really didn't know anything about him (other than his taste in women), I found myself wondering how he put up with Glenn as a business partner.

"I have a trust fund," I said, immediately recognizing the expression in his eyes—"Oh, so that's where she got her money." I paused to take a breath, even though part of me had to admit he wasn't exactly wrong. Yes, my tea business paid the bills, but it would be far more challenging for me without the trust fund. "While the person who manages it is based in New York, since I'm here to stay, I thought it might make sense to also look for someone local to manage part of it."

He was busy with his notes. "Yes, that is definitely something we can help with. I'll need a few details."

He asked a bunch of questions, which I did my best to answer in a way that sounded more promising than the situation was. Truth be told, there was really no way Mr. Farley would ever give up one iota of control.

When he was satisfied with my answers to his questions, he leaned back in his chair to give me his little sales pitch: how long he's been in business, how many satisfied customers he had, and what I could expect working with him.

I smiled and nodded during his little spiel, and when he was finished, he asked if I had any questions.

"Not really," I said. "You came highly recommended."

He smiled wide, revealing a lot of teeth. "Can I ask who? We love rewarding happy clients."

"Of course. It was my client, Courtney Fallon."

His smile faded a little, and he suddenly became very busy straightening up his desk. "Well, that's sweet, that she did that. I'm sure you must have heard about her husband."

"I did," I said.

"I'm surprised you came in now after what, err, happened."

"Well, to be frank, I meant to come in earlier," I said, flashing him an embarrassed smile as I lied through my teeth. "But, with the new year, I thought it would be smart to make the move. However," I continued, and Glenn's expression, which had started to relax, tensed up again. "I *was* wondering how you were handling things, in light of Dennis's death."

"An excellent question," Glenn said, although the stiffness of his body screamed otherwise. "I can assure you that, as a client, there will be no issues on your end. Of course, we will have a transition here, and I already have feelers out for a new financial advisor to take his place, but I can promise you that we will do everything in our power to make our team transitions as painless and seamless as possible for you."

I smiled. "That's great to hear. I'm glad you're already on top of things. It must have been a huge shock when it happened. No one would blame you if you needed to take some time off to grieve and regroup."

Glenn smoothed his tie again. "Yes, it was a shock," he said. "I suppose that's the case when anyone dies. My father was sick for a long time, and even though we expected his death, when it happened, it was still a shock. Under these circumstances, it's especially so. I thought about shutting the business down for a few days, but quite honestly, working helps me. I know if I were sitting at home, all I would be doing is thinking about the business anyway, and how to move forward with Dennis gone." He gave me a thin smile, but I could see the tension and stress behind it. "Plus, this time of year is always busy, so it's better to keep working."

I nodded, my expression understanding. "I can imagine how difficult all this is for you. I'm having trouble getting my head around what happened, and I never even met Dennis. And while I'm not especially close with Courtney, I personally can't believe she had anything to do with his death."

Glenn's smile froze. He started fiddling with the items on his desk again, shifting them and moving them around. "How well do we know anyone, really?" he asked. "Aren't we all capable of violence under the right circumstances?" He glanced at me then, his expression embarrassed, as if suddenly realizing I was still in the room. "Sorry," he said. "Clearly, I'm not myself. I've known Courtney since the beginning of their relationship. I was even the best man at their wedding. It's been ..." he paused, shaking his head, his fingers continuously rearranging items, as if they had a mind of their own. "Difficult."

I nodded again, making sure I kept my face arranged in a compassionate-yet- interested expression. "Was their marriage troubled?"

"What marriage isn't?" He must have seen something in my face, because he forced a smile. "I just mean, it's difficult to really know what's going on inside a marriage when you're on the outside looking in. On the surface, they seemed happy enough, but ..." he shrugged.

"Do you know any reason Courtney might have had for wanting to hurt Dennis?" I watched him closely. He must know about Dennis's affair. I couldn't believe as his business partner, he wouldn't have noticed something—long lunches, leaving early, working late. Maybe Tiffany even came by the office a few times for a quickie on the desk.

Glenn stopped fiddling and straightened up, smoothing his tie and folding his hands on his desk. "I'm sure the police will sort it out," he said dismissively. "Do you have any other questions for me about our services?" It appeared we were done talking about Dennis and Courtney.

"Mr. Haggard?" The secretary cracked open the door and poked her head in. She was probably around my age with short, dark hair, dark eyes, and a thin mouth that a heavy coat of red lipstick couldn't completely mask. "Mr. Christof is on the phone for you again."

Glenn pressed his lips together. "Not now, June. Can't you see I'm with someone?"

"But he was very insistent ..."

"Not now," Glenn snapped. "Tell him I'll call him back when I'm done with my meeting."

"Of course, Mr. Haggard," June murmured, her expression reminding me of a kicked dog. She slunk out of the office, closing the door behind her.

Glenn straightened up. "I apologize for that," he said. "As you can imagine, it's been an adjustment for everyone, including our clients. While it's normal for people to want to make sure all will be well when it comes to their money, a few of them have been quite concerned. We're doing our best to reassure them as much as possible, but it's going to take some time."

"Of course," I said. "I understand."

He smiled a tiny smile. "So, do you have any other questions?"

I shook my head. "No, you've been very helpful. And you've given me a lot to think about."

"Let me know if you think of any others."

I reached down to collect my purse when my eye caught the framed photograph. During Glenn's fiddling, he had shifted it, so I could now see who it was—a woman with carefully styled blonde hair, perfect makeup, and intense green eyes.

I had to blink a few times, sure I was seeing things. It couldn't be her.

It just couldn't.

"Mrs., err, Ms. Kingsley? Is everything all right?" Glenn was staring at me, his expression concerned.

My mouth had gone dry. "Sorry. I just ... is that your wife?"

Glenn glanced at where I was pointing. "Ah, yes. That's Tiffany."

"She's ... she's lovely," I said faintly, but inside, I was screaming. Dennis was sleeping with his business partner's wife? That couldn't be right. Violet must have gotten the names mixed up. Surely, this information was too important not to share with me, had she known.

Glenn beamed. "She is, isn't she? She owns a health and fitness club here in town. Fit for Life. Have you been there?"

I swallowed. "Yes, actually. I was thinking about getting a membership for the new year. You know, a New Year's resolution."

"Ah, yes. You would definitely be in good company."

I stood up, wanting nothing more than to get out of that stuffy, sparse office. "Thank you for your time. I'll be in touch."

Glenn stood as well, reaching across the desk to shake my hand. "It was nice meeting you, Ms. Kingsley. I trust you won't let our current ... well, 'troubles,' dissuade you from using our services."

His hand was hot and heavy, and his grip was tight. Uncomfortably tight. Like he was purposefully squeezing my hand. His eyes had a strange glint to them, and I was suddenly aware of how alone we were. June's desk was down the hall and near the front door. With the door closed, would she even hear me if I screamed?

I pulled my hand away. "Of course not," I said. "It's not like it was your fault Dennis died. Right?"

I couldn't believe the words had come out of my mouth. *Charlie*, a little voice snapped inside of me. *Are you trying to get yourself in trouble?*

Glenn also seemed in disbelief. His eyes widened, and his jaw dropped open. We started at each other in silence for a moment before I forced myself to laugh.

"Sorry," I said. "Just a bad joke. I shouldn't have said it."

Glenn's mustache twitched as he frowned in disapproval. "No, you shouldn't have."

"I'll ... um ... I'll just go." I turned and hurried down the hallway, forcing myself not to run.

Are you out of your mind? The little voice hissed at me. *If he IS Dennis's murderer, do you really think antagonizing him was a smart move?*

While the little voice had a point, what I saw in Glenn's eyes was worth the risk.

There was something underneath the shock. Something that shouldn't have been there if he were completely innocent.

Fear.

Chapter 8

"Hold on," Pat said, holding her hands out as if she could physically stop the flow of words from my mouth. "Dennis was having an affair with his business partner's wife?"

I yanked the Tupperware container out of the cupboard, spraying flour into the air like a white cloud. When I was upset, I baked. "Don't you think that would have been good information to have shared with me?" I asked, presumably to Pat, but I could have just as well been talking to the stick of butter sitting on the counter waiting to be turned into gingerbread, or Midnight, who had meandered into the kitchen and was sitting by his bowl.

I had called Violet the moment I walked in my house. Violet's response: "You mean you didn't know Tiffany is Glenn's wife?"

"How could I have?" I demanded.

"Well, I just figured you knew."

"They have different last names," I nearly shouted.

"Oh, oh," Violet said, suddenly sounding lost and confused. "I just ... it's such a blur. Was it important to tell you?"

I clamped my jaw together and forced myself to count to ten as I paced around the kitchen as far as the cord would go. *She's an old woman,* I reminded myself, *and her daughter, her pregnant daughter, is suspected of killing her husband. Of course she isn't thinking straight.* "If I'm going to help you, I need to know everything," I said. "Otherwise, I could screw something up and not even know it."

"Oh, of course. That makes sense," Violet said. "I should have thought of that. Forgive me."

"It's fine," I said. "Just please don't hide things from me."

"Did you say anything to Courtney?" There was an edge to her voice that hadn't been there before.

"What does that matter?" I asked.

"Does that mean you didn't?"

"No, I didn't say anything to Courtney. Why?"

Violet let out a sigh of relief. "She doesn't like talking about it, as you can imagine. It really upsets her. And she's upset enough right now. I told her I'd handle it. So, if you wouldn't mind ..." Her voice trailed off.

"I won't say anything," I said. "But that means you need to be honest with me. Is there anything else I should know?"

Her voice was hesitant. "I ... I don't think so. But let me think about it and get back to you."

I hung up, sure she still wasn't telling me everything. But what was she hiding? And why?

"So, why didn't they tell you?"

I grabbed the sugar out of the cupboard and nearly dropped it. I had forgotten I had just filled it, so it was much heavier. "Violet thought I knew."

Pat looked perplexed. "But how would you? Their last names are different."

I pointed my wooden spoon at Pat. "Yes! My point exactly."

Pat shook her head as she picked up her tea. "This is really bizarre. Maybe Courtney is guilty after all."

I plucked the baking soda out of the cupboard with a lot less force than before. "Maybe. But Glenn sure was acting like he had something to hide. And he had motive, as well. Just as much as Courtney."

"You're assuming Glenn knows about Dennis and his wife."

And just like that, all my anger and frustration drained out of me. I slumped against the counter, letting out a deep sigh. "That's true. I just don't know what to do," I said. "Maybe it was an honest mistake. Violet is pretty upset and isn't thinking straight. Or maybe she was embarrassed. I mean, it's embarrassing that her son-in-law was cheating on her daughter with his business partner's wife. Or maybe she really didn't think it was that important. So, it's possible her not telling me really doesn't mean anything. But ..." I chewed on my lip.

Pat raised an eyebrow. "You think it does?"

"It seems suspicious," I said. "Not to mention I think there's more she didn't tell me. She asked me to help her, so why is she keeping secrets? Doesn't that seem suspicious to you?"

Pat shrugged. "I don't know. You could be right about why Violet didn't tell you. Should it be considered 'suspicious?' Maybe, but maybe not. As for other stuff she's hiding, everyone has things they would prefer others don't know. It could be just something embarrassing or dumb they did when they were younger. But again, not necessarily criminal, or even something to be concerned about."

"But you and I both felt like Courtney was hiding something when we talked to her," I said.

"It's like you said before. What would be the point of intentionally not telling you? Especially since you would likely find out."

I went back to my baking. "Maybe to confuse things?" I guessed. "I mean, if Courtney really is guilty, maybe Violet is hoping I do mess things up. That would make it more difficult for the cops to make a case against Courtney."

"I think you're reaching," Pat said.

"You're probably right," I agreed. "Especially since *everyone* seems to be acting guilty. Glenn sure seemed like he was hiding something. And Tiffany is clearly not happy in her marriage."

"Well, if you want my two cents, at this point, I would probably assume Violet not telling you was an innocent mistake and take a much harder look at Tiffany and Glenn. Especially Glenn."

"Yeah, Glenn has certainly moved to the top of my list of suspects now that I know he had motive," I said. "He had the means, too. He would have known Dennis's favorite brandy. He would have known about Arthur, the cousin. Heck, he probably would have even known that they weren't going to the Christmas Eve party, so he would have had the opportunity to set it up to look like Courtney did it."

"But that brings up another point—why would he do that to Courtney?" Pat asked. "Wasn't she as much a victim as he was? Why would he do that to her?"

"That's true." I hadn't thought about that angle, and I mulled it over as I started my KitchenAid mixer and dug the loaf pan out of the cabinet. "Maybe he didn't mean to set her up. Maybe it was an accident."

Pat raised an eyebrow. "He set her up by accident?"

"Yeah, I mean, it's possible. We still don't know what he was poisoned with," I said. "Maybe Glenn used something that he thought would mimic a natural death. Let's not forget, Courtney did think he had a heart attack."

"You think Glenn would have been stupid enough to believe the cops wouldn't test the brandy?"

I shrugged. "Who knows what he thought? Maybe he didn't think it would happen that quickly. If Dennis had collapsed after he put the bottle away, maybe the cops would have assumed he died from natural causes. Then, they wouldn't test the brandy."

"Sounds a bit like reaching again."

I poured the batter into the loaf pan. "Glenn is a financial advisor, not a doctor. He would have no idea what he was doing, in that respect, and it wasn't like he was in the room with Dennis. It's also possible he thought that because the brandy showed up as a gift, the cops would assume it was someone other than Courtney. Why would Courtney go through all the trouble of packaging up a bottle of brandy and sending it as a gift? She could just quietly poison something in the house."

"Which would lead back to her," Pat pointed out.

"Maybe, maybe not," I countered. "It depends on what she did. Like, for instance, if she poisoned him slowly, over time, it might just look like he got really sick and never recovered."

Pat shivered. "That would take nerves of steel, to watch someone slowly die."

I thought about Courtney, and how she could barely hold it together when we had visited her. "Yeah, I don't think she could do it either," I said. "But there's other ways you can kill someone without poisoning him. Make it look like an accident."

"That's true, but what if Courtney is counting on that?" Pat asked. "That people would assume if it were her, she would have done it differently. And that's exactly why she chose this method."

I popped the gingerbread into the oven. "I suppose that's possible, too." I shook my head and picked up my tea.

Pat gave me a sympathetic look. "How will you figure it out?"

"I guess I keep digging," I said. "I'm working on setting up a meeting with Nina. I left her a voicemail, but she hasn't responded. And I'm seeing Tiffany tomorrow to talk about supplying tea to Fit for Life. In fact, this is the tea I created for it. Do you like?" I held up the mug.

She took another swallow. "Ah, I thought it was new. It's good. So, this is the post-workout tea?"

"Yep," I said. "It's designed to help with muscle soreness and inflammation."

Pat took another sip, then leaned over to prop her elbows on the counter. "You know, you're probably going to lose her as a client once she figures out what you're really after."

"Which is why I tested it on you," I said. "I figured if it's any good, I can sell it myself."

Chapter 9

"So sorry to keep you waiting," Tiffany said, peeling off a pair of bright-yellow rubber gloves as she breezed into the closet that doubled as an office. Her hair was slicked back into a ponytail, and she had a smudge of something on her chin. She gave me a quick smile before squeezing behind her overflowing desk. Tiffany definitely used the "pile" method of organization. Mounds of paper were everywhere, including on the chair underneath me. When Jillian showed me to Tiffany's office, she told me to "put the pile anywhere." The only problem was that there wasn't really "anywhere" to put it, as the only empty spaces appeared to be the walkway. But then I realized the space under my chair was empty, so I shoved the pile there.

"No problem," I said. "You have something here," I added, gesturing toward my own chin.

She stared at me, then touched her skin. "Oh, it's a piece of wet paper towel." She brushed it away, smudging her pink lipstick in the process. "I was doing a little cleaning. I hate leaving it all 'til the end of the day, as I'm usually tired then. Trying to get it all done at that point can be overwhelming."

Cleaning? Didn't she have a cleaning service? While I got the fact that you wear a lot of hats as a business owner, being the janitor, too, seemed a little much.

She must have seen something in my face, because she continued talking. "It's only temporary. My last cleaning service wasn't working out, so we parted ways a month ago. You wouldn't believe how difficult it is to find someone new during the holiday season, so I figured it was just easier for me to handle it until I could look for someone when the new year started."

"I guess people want their evenings free for holiday parties," I said.

She flashed me another smile. "Yeah, that's probably it. Anyway, I'm so glad you're here. I've been excited to talk with you."

"Me too. In fact," I pulled out the little bag from my purse. "I brought you some tea to try."

Her face lit up. "Oh! I love that. Let me just heat up some water. I'll be back in a jiff." She meandered her way between the piles, and I had to admire how well she was able to navigate. Maybe all the aerobics classes really do pay off.

She brought back two mugs of sort-of-hot water. I made a mental note to have a conversation with her about an easier way to get hotter water. She was also going to need more tea infusers, as all my tea was loose. I had brought only one with me, so I used it for her cup. "I have another one around here somewhere," she fretted, looking around the office.

"Don't worry about it," I said. "I've already tasted it."

She gave me a sideways smile. "One of these days, I'll clean up in here. I always intend to, but there are just never enough hours in the day."

I smiled reassuringly. "I get it."

While we waited for the tea to steep, she explained her proposal. I would sell on consignment, with a 60/40 split (she would get the 60). I would be in charge of regularly checking in and keeping inventory stocked, whereas she would handle collecting the money.

"So, if people want to make a cup of tea and sit in the lobby, how will that work?" I asked.

She took another sip of hers, which she clearly loved. "What do you mean?"

"Well, I thought that was part of what you wanted—a place for your clients to enjoy a cup of tea after their workout."

"Oh, yes." She frowned. " It would have to be self-service. I guess I could offer some paper cups … "

"So, you'll need a way for people to get hot water," I said. "And you'll probably want to offer other fixings, too, like fresh lemon, honey, and cream. And you'll need tea infusers."

The more I talked, the more her face seemed to close down. "That's a lot of work," she said, her voice hesitant. "Especially when we don't even know if it will sell or not. What if we just sold packages they could take home?"

"We could certainly start with that," I said. "That's probably smart. To test out the concept."

Her smile was relieved.

"Of course," I continued. "Sales would be better if we could have them taste it first. I've found providing a sample sells the tea itself."

Her smile faded. "That makes sense," she said. "I don't know, but I was hoping this would be really simple to start. I'm just so busy with everything."

"We can keep it simple," I said, even though her reluctance puzzled me. Hadn't she realized all that would be involved in selling tea to her customers? Or had she just not given it much thought at all? "If you do ever want to start selling cups, you might want to think about offering coffee, as well. I know you didn't want to, but a coffee maker would also heat the water for you, so it would make sense to have both."

"Yeah, you have a good point. I'll look into it. Anything else?"

I actually did have more questions—the 60-40 split, for one—as it seemed like I would be the one doing all the work and shouldering the expenses. But her whole demeanor was so strange. The conversation was not going at all like I'd expected.

Normally, I would have waited until she was in a better mood before I brought up her husband, but watching her energy level plummet, I wasn't sure if I would get another chance to talk to her privately. "Not about the tea, at least for right now," I said, plastering a smile across my face. "But I *did* want to tell you … I met your husband."

Her eyes grew wide. "You met Glenn?" Her voice was strained, and she seemed shocked.

I bobbed my head up and down. "Yep. I'm looking for a financial advisor. I had a meeting with him yesterday."

"A meeting?" She had gone from shocked to flustered. "How did you know I'm married to him?"

"He has a framed picture of you in his office," I said. "I was surprised, because you two don't have the same last name."

She chuckled, but it sounded a little forced. "When we got married, I was pretty established under my own name. Plus, I never really loved the idea of women having to change their names when they marry."

"Established?"

"I was working as a model," she said.

"Wow. A model. How exciting."

She laughed, and it sounded much more natural. "Not really. A lot of hurry up and wait. Plus, being photographed for hours can get old pretty quickly. But I still enjoyed it." Her face had a faraway look. "I knew it wouldn't be forever, so I thought rather than try and build everything back up with a new last name, I would just keep going with my maiden name. I figured I could change it later, like if we had kids … but unfortunately, that doesn't seem to be in the cards." Her eyes were sad.

"Sorry," I said, feeling a little pang of sadness myself. There was a time when I thought I was going to have it all: the husband, the 2.5 kids, the white picket fence … but it didn't end up working out that way.

She gave her head a quick shake. "Nothing to be sorry about. Clearly, it's not meant to be." She gave me a faint smile.

A part of me wanted to ask her more questions, but it didn't seem like she wanted to talk about it. "Well, Glenn was great," I said. "It must be nice having a financial advisor as a husband. You don't have to worry about any of that. And didn't he lend you the money, as well? That was nice. I mean, not having to go through a bank."

"Yeah, I am grateful for the loan. And he does take care of all the finances. Our personal as well as the business's. So yes, it's nice to have those tasks off my plate."

She shifted in her chair, like she was done with the conversation and ready for me to leave. I quickly plowed on, before she could make an excuse about getting back to work. "I was surprised he was taking appointments, though."

Her lips curled down. "You're talking about what happened to his business partner." Her voice was flat.

"Yes. It was really shocking to read about in the paper. I mean, it was a shock for me, and I've never met Dennis. Just his wife ..."

"You know Courtney?" Tiffany blurted out, interrupting me. Under her makeup, her face had gone pale.

"Yes, she's my client," I said.

"Your *client*?"

"Yes, she buys my teas." I cocked my head and studied her. "Is there a problem? Do you not like her?"

Tiffany had collapsed into her chair. "I just ... I didn't realize you knew her."

"Redemption is a small town," I said. "It might be more unusual if I didn't know her." I smiled, trying to lighten the mood.

Tiffany didn't smile back, instead picking up her tea and cupping her hands around it as if for warmth. "I'm sorry. My reaction was probably pretty confusing. It's been tough, as you can imagine. I've ... we've known Dennis for years. It's been such a shock."

"I can imagine," I said. "I'm just amazed at how well the two of you are holding up."

She gave me a twisted smile. "It's not always easy, believe me. I've had my moments. But for the most part, I've discovered that working helps keep my mind off things, which is good, because with the holidays, I'm even more short-staffed than usual. So, I really have to work."

I wondered about her being more short-staffed than usual. There was something there. I could feel it, but I also didn't want to lose the opportunity to ask about her relationship with Courtney and Dennis, so I mentally filed it away to deal with later.

"So, you knew Courtney as well, right?" I asked.

"Of course. Actually, I was the reason Courtney and Dennis met."

I nearly fell off my chair. It was all I could do to keep a straight face. "Really?" I asked, hoping Tiffany hadn't noticed whatever crazy, shocked expression was surely on my face. Would I ever get to the bottom of the surprises in this case?

"Yeah," Tiffany said. "She was one of my aerobics instructors. One evening, Glenn and I were going to a work dinner with Dennis. Glenn was going to pick me up here, so I didn't have to waste time driving home to change. For some reason, Dennis came with him. Actually, now that I think about it, Dennis was having car trouble, so Glenn was going to give him a ride. Anyway, Courtney had finished her class and was leaving as Dennis and Glenn arrived. I wasn't quite ready yet, so Dennis and Courtney ended up chatting for a few minutes, and that was all it took." She shrugged and smiled, but it wasn't a happy one. "Dennis found out when Courtney was teaching next and showed up to ask her out. It was a whirlwind courtship, and then, they were engaged."

"Wow," I said. "That's kind of romantic."

"I guess it was love at first sight." She started playing with her cardboard cup, swirling the tea around. "As you can imagine, we did a lot of double dating, both before they were married and after. And Glenn was Dennis's best man at his wedding."

"This must be awful for you," I offered. "Especially knowing them the way you did. And, especially with what the cops are saying ..." My voice trailed off.

Tiffany eyed me. "What about the cops?"

I leaned forward slightly and lowered my voice, like we were two old friends about to indulge in a good gossip. "They think Courtney was the one who killed Dennis. Can you imagine? Courtney? I can't picture it, especially in her condition. But I also haven't known her very long. Can I ask what you think? If you don't want to talk about it, I understand, but it's really been bothering me. I mean, a client of mine maybe being a murderer, and I didn't even know it ..."

Tiffany glanced away, seeming to focus instead on another inspirational poster hanging on the wall—yet another cat, and the words "When life leaves you hanging, DON'T QUIT."

"I know how you feel," she said in a low voice. "I'm having trouble believing it, as well. Especially when I think about all the time we spent together, having them over to our house for dinner, eating at their house." She shivered. "Was it the pregnancy hormones? Did she just snap?"

I stared at her, trying to process what it was that I was hearing. "So you think Courtney did it?"

She must have heard something in my voice, because she quickly started backtracking. "Well, I don't actually know," she admitted. "But it just seems really suspicious. Dennis poisoned? By his favorite brandy? How many people even know about his favorite brandy? Or his cousin? It would have to be someone close to him."

"Can you think of anyone else?" I asked. "You knew Dennis a long time. Maybe he had a falling out with a friend or family member? Or maybe a disgruntled client?"

She was shaking her head. "Everyone loved Dennis. He handled most of the networking and meeting and greeting." She smiled as she talked, a different smile than any I'd seen so far. It softened her face and brought out her beauty in a way that all the thick makeup failed to do. "Glenn is ... well, you met him. He's the numbers guy. He's a little more ... buttoned up, than Dennis ever was. Which made them a good team, because Glenn dealt mostly with the numbers, and Dennis dealt mostly with the clients. I don't know what's going to happen with Dennis gone." She bit her lip and turned away, but not before I saw a sheen of tears in her eyes.

Tiffany had real feelings for Dennis. That shocked me a little, even though it shouldn't. If they were having an affair, then it made sense. But still, the idea that she was in love with her husband's married business partner felt messed up ... like witnessing an episode of *Jerry Springer*.

"Is the business doing well?" I asked. I wasn't sure what prompted that question. Based on Courtney's house and that she apparently didn't work, I assumed it was. But, based on Tiffany's reaction, it appeared I hit a nerve. She snapped her head around to stare at me, nearly knocking her piles of paper to the ground.

"Why would you ask such a question?" Her voice was high, too high, and she paused to take a breath.

"I ... I didn't mean anything by it," I said. "I guess I was still thinking about the disgruntled client scenario. Maybe an investment didn't turn out as planned, and some clients got upset or something."

Her eyes grew wide. "You think an investment not going well would lead to murder?" Her voice was still too high, and suddenly, all the strange little things I'd been noticing came together like an image from a kaleidoscope.

Tiffany not having enough staff, even having to do her own cleaning. Her reluctance to buy the supplies needed to sell the tea. Her membership sale, and how quick she was to push me to sign up.

Tiffany was having money problems.

And, just as clearly, Glenn was refusing to give her another loan.

I wondered why. Was it because Tiffany wasn't a good businesswoman, and Glenn didn't want to dump good money after bad? Or because his business wasn't doing well, either, and he didn't have the money to give?

Or was he lying to Tiffany, telling her the business wasn't doing well because he didn't want to tell her the truth about why he didn't want to give her a loan?

"Um ... well, I thought the two biggest motivations for murder were love and money," I said. "Clearly, it's not a healthy reaction, but people aren't always thinking clearly in those moments."

"It still seems extreme," she insisted.

More than a wife murdering a husband? I wanted to ask, but then again, there is a reason cops look at the spouse first when foul play is suspected. And usually, at the end of the day, the spouse IS the guilty one.

"I agree, it does seem extreme," I said. I'm just throwing out people other than Courtney who might have done it. As far as I can tell, Courtney didn't have much of a motive. I thought she and Dennis were happy. She said they never fought. Or is that not true? Was there a problem with their marriage?"

As I spoke, I closely studied Tiffany's face. From the little I knew about her, she was pretty much an open book, her feelings clearly revealed on her face.

She probably knew that, too, because she turned away from me. "If there was a problem, I wasn't aware of it either," she said softly. "They always seemed happy to me. Of course, who knows what goes on inside a marriage … especially when you're on the outside looking in."

I sucked in a quick breath of air. Glenn had said almost the exact same thing. It made me wonder which marriage they were talking about—Dennis and Courtney's, or their own?

I also couldn't figure out if she was telling the truth or lying. Her eyes were turned away, still staring at the DON'T QUIT message, no doubt. But, if she was telling the truth, why would Dennis cheat?

And what would be the purpose of lying? The whole conversation seemed to be about throwing Courtney under the bus. So why not share the juicy gossip about the marriage being in trouble?

Nothing about this case made sense.

Suddenly, she started. "Oh, look at the time. I have to go." She jumped to her feet and started weaving her way to the door.

I stood, as well. "So, the tea …."

"Yes, yes, just bring in some bags, and let's see if we can sell it," she said, practically pushing me out the door. There was a flustered, frantic energy about her, and she was careful not to look at me. "Don't bring in a lot, though. Just enough to test the concept. Sound like a plan?"

"Sure," I said, even though I still didn't like the split. Although honestly, did it even matter? Bringing in a few bags of tea would be the perfect opportunity to continue this conversation after doing a little more digging on my end. And chances were, the more questions I kept asking, the less likely Tiffany was to want anything to do with me, so any tea-selling opportunity would disappear anyhow. "I'll be back once I get the bags together."

Her smile was perfunctory. "Great." She turned to walk away, still talking to me over her shoulder. "Just stop by. If I'm not around, Jillian can help you."

I watched her disappear into the aerobics room. I suspected I had one, maybe two more conversations with her before she was done.

I was definitely was going to have to make the next one count.

Chapter 10

I finished parking my car alongside the curb, turned the engine off, and paused for a moment, staring at Courtney's house.

I knew Pat would be furious with me for going without her, but there were answers I needed from Courtney, and I had a feeling I would be more likely to get them alone.

I also had a feeling that I might be more successful with this meeting if I had the element of surprise.

I was tired of finding out vital information about Courtney from other people. Something needed to give. And since I didn't want to go through her mother, I needed to talk to her directly.

But still, I paused. I was used to people dropping by unexpectedly—it kind of came with the territory of operating a business out of a home. But it wasn't the norm for most. I also had to keep reminding myself that Courtney was not only very pregnant, but grieving.

The polite, compassionate move would be to call and see if she was okay with seeing a visitor.

However, after learning that Tiffany was not only Glenn's wife, but also Courtney's former boss, I was feeling less than charitable.

I got out of the car and headed up the driveway. If she wasn't there, or if she wasn't in a good frame of mind to talk, I would leave and make an appointment with her for a different time, I told myself.

But I wanted to try this first.

The house was quiet as I approached, making me question whether she was home. I stepped onto the porch and rang the doorbell. As I stood there waiting for her to answer, I mentally sent Pat an apology and promised to tell her everything.

For a moment, there was silence, making me think again that I would have to call to arrange a time to talk to her, but then, I heard faint footsteps before the door cracked open.

"Charlie?"

My eyes widened in shock as I looked at her, although I tried to cover it up. She looked awful. Her face was way too thin, her cheeks hollowed out and an almost greenish tint to her skin. This couldn't be good for the baby. Looking at her, I started to question the wisdom in asking her a bunch of uncomfortable and likely unwelcome questions.

On the other hand, if she ended up getting charged with murder, her life was going to get about twenty times more stressful than anything I could do to her. If she wanted my help, whatever games she was playing had to stop. Now.

"How are you doing?" Even as I asked, the words sounded ridiculous. Obviously, she wasn't doing well. You only needed eyes to see it. But societal norms are deeply engrained.

She forced a smile. "I've been better. Did you want to come in?" She held the door open a little wider.

"Just as long as I'm not bothering you," I said as I stepped through.

"No bother," she answered, her voice quiet and a little wistful. "I wouldn't mind a little company."

Another pang of guilt shot through me. I should have been more attentive ... should have stopped by sooner and not waited until I had an agenda. But too late now. "How is the baby?"

She smiled, a true smile, and pressed a hand against her belly. "Kicking away. I think he might be a soccer player."

I raised an eyebrow. "He?"

Her smile turned mischievous. "None of the doctors told me, if that's what you're asking. I just have a feeling. Do you want anything to drink? Coffee? Tea? Water?"

"I'm fine ... you don't need to trouble yourself," I said, taking my coat off.

"It's no trouble. I was thinking about making myself a cup of tea." There was something about how she was standing there looking at me, an almost desperate eagerness to please in her energy, that broke my heart.

"Tea would be great," I said. "It's nippy out there. A nice cup would do the trick."

Her smile was relieved. "I have just enough of your Candy Cane Concoctions for one more pot. I save it for special occasions, but even so, I'm almost out. It's so good."

"I can bring you more," I said, kicking myself for not having thought to do so. "I also have some great blends for expectant and new mothers I can bring by."

Her eyes lit up. "That would be great. Do you want to go sit in the living room? I've got a fire going."

"You don't want any help with the tea?"

She waved her hand, brushing me off. "No, no. I've got it. Go sit by the fire and relax."

She moved into the kitchen, a hand on her lower back, and I went to do as she said.

The living room was in much better shape than the last time. The papers on the coffee table had been put away, and the room had signs of recent dusting and vacuuming. I wondered if Courtney was doing it herself, or if she had someone helping her … maybe her mother. Someone had also put all the Christmas decorations away, which made me sad for some reason. I wondered again if her child would grow up never enjoying Christmas because of what happened this season.

"Here we go," Courtney said as she entered the room. She was carrying a tray loaded with the tea pot and mugs, and with every step, the pot rattled. I quickly got up to take the tray from her.

"Thanks. I looked for some cookies, but I guess the baby must have been hungry," she said, trying to joke.

"That's okay," I quickly assured her. "Trust me, I eat enough baked goods on my own. I don't need any more."

I set the tray down on the coffee table as Courtney lowered herself into the chair in front of me. I poured both mugs and handed one to her. She accepted hers, and we both took a sip.

"So, my mother tells me you're helping find out the truth," Courtney said.

I set the mug down on the table. "I'm certainly trying."

She looked up at me, her clear, china-blue eyes reminding me so much of a child. "Thank you," she said. "I really appreciate it. And if you need money ..."

I shook my head. "No, no. I'm fine. It's not like I'm a professional at this or anything."

"Well, if you need anything," she said. "Anything at all, I'm here for you. Have you come to give me an update? Should I call my mother, as well?" She started moving, as if to head toward the phone, but I held my hand out.

"Hold on. Yes, I'm here for an update, but I also have some additional questions, too. Maybe we bring your mother in later. If you want."

Courtney slowly lowered herself back into her chair, her expression wary. "Questions?"

I gave her what I hoped was a reassuring smile. "So, I spoke to both Glenn and Tiffany."

I paused, watching her closely to see if she reacted to Tiffany's name. Even though I had promised Violet I wouldn't bring it up, I was hoping for an opening, so I could talk to her about it.

But Courtney didn't seem to react, other than dropping her gaze to look down at her hands.

"I didn't realize that Tiffany was your former boss, or that you met Dennis through her," I continued, deciding to skip the cheating for now.

Courtney remained silent, still staring at her hands. Her blonde hair had fallen across her face like a curtain at the end of an act, so I couldn't even get a look at her expression.

I stayed quiet as well, waiting her out. The silence stretched longer than I expected, making me wonder if she was ever going to break it.

Finally, she stirred, lifting her head so her hair fell away. "We ... I should have told you," she said softly.

"Why didn't you?"

She looked down again. "I'm not really sure. I guess ... I was ashamed."

I didn't expect that response. Was Dennis still married when he got together with Courtney? "Why would you be ashamed?"

"I guess ..." she bit her lip. "I always felt a little guilty about how Dennis and I met," she said in a rush.

Immediately, I started thinking back to the conversation with Tiffany, trying to remember if she had talked about Dennis's marital status. I didn't recall anything, which of course didn't mean he was single. "Why?"

She let out a heavy sigh, almost as if that statement alone was causing a deeply buried secret to emerge. "It's a long story," she said.

"I have plenty of time," I replied, making a point of sitting back in my chair, as if settling in for the long haul. I was getting the feeling that whatever she was going to confess had been troubling her for a very long time.

She looked down into her tea again, as if searching it for strength, before finally beginning to speak. "When I was thirteen, my father had a midlife crisis and ran off with a younger woman. A MUCH younger woman. My mother was devastated. It completely blindsided her emotionally, of course, but even more than that, it was financially devastating. My mother hadn't had a job in years, since before I was born. She had no real job skills, no prospects, no nothing. It was awful. The only job she could get was low-paying temp work through an agency. We had to move out of our beautiful home and into a dreadful apartment. The walls were so thin, I could hear her crying after I went to bed every night. It was just awful."

"But what about the courts? Didn't your father have to pay alimony and child support?"

"When I say, 'ran off,' I mean literally," she said bitterly. "One day, he drained our bank accounts and vanished with that woman. Cops were no help, because it's not against the law to disappear when you're an adult. And we didn't have the money to hire a private investigator to find him. If you don't know where he is, you can't get money from him."

"What about family? Could they help you financially?"

She sighed. "My mother's parents did what they could, but they were living on a fixed income themselves. On my dad's side, his mother was in a nursing home and had dementia, so she wasn't much help, and his father wasn't in the picture. He never talked much about his father, but I got the sense that his dad had left his mother much like he left us." She paused, as she swirled the tea in her cup. "His mother died a few years ago. I think, of all the things my father did to us, that's the one thing my mother really found unforgivable. That he left his mother like that. We continued to visit her until the day she died, and she never stopped asking about my father. It was ..." she shook her head.

"Anyway, I helped as much as I could, but I was only thirteen when it happened, so I couldn't get a real job. I did other things ... helped around the house, babysat, got a paper route, and did other odd jobs. Whatever I could do to help earn a little money.

"When I turned sixteen, I got my first real job, cleaning offices and commercial buildings at night. My mother didn't want me to do it. She wanted me to focus on school, but she also knew we needed the money. By then, she was working two jobs and still barely able to make ends meet. She wanted to go back to school ... maybe study to become a nurse, so she could get a decent-paying job. She was always interested in health, medicine, and natural remedies and whatnot. But there was no time or money for that, either. Anyway, eventually, we reached an agreement that I could take this job as long as it didn't impact my studies.

"Needless to say, that didn't last long. I took as many shifts as they would give me, which of course cut into school, and after a few weeks, I dropped out. My mother didn't find out for several months, mostly because neither of us were home very much. She was furious." Courtney grimaced at the memory. "I told her it was temporary. I could work multiple jobs for a while, which would free her up to go back to school. Once she had a decent job, I could go back and get my GED and figure out what I wanted to do. She didn't like that plan at all. She thought it made more sense for me to get my schooling and a good job, but I told her that would take longer, since I still had to finish high school. It made more sense for her to go first. Plus, I was younger and didn't mind working multiple jobs. She wasn't happy about it, but at that point, there was nothing she could really do. I had quit several months before, so there was no going back.

"Fast forward a few years later, and Tiffany hires me to man the front desk on weekends. It was a bad time for me. I was exhausted. I had been working 60-70- hour weeks for years by then, in mostly menial jobs like waitressing and cleaning, and it was exhausting. My mother was in nursing school, and it was going a lot slower than either of us had anticipated. It was a huge adjustment for her to become a student again after so many years. Plus, she was still working full-time as a temp on top of her studies, so it was just ... well, difficult. *Everything* felt difficult. I was feeling really beat down and discouraged with life. At that moment, I couldn't see a way out of the slog of working all the time I had found myself in. I was feeling very sorry for myself.

"It was during this time that I started to get to know Tiffany. Working at Fit for Life was becoming the bright spot of my week. I got to sit at a desk all weekend, which felt like heaven, and the little bit of cleaning, straightening, and organizing I was supposed to do was so easy compared to my other jobs. I was flying through it and even doing extra tasks, just because it was easy for me. And I didn't mind.

"Well, Tiffany noticed I was going above and beyond and started stopping in on the weekends to talk to me. I guess we became friends, in a way, if you can even be friends with your boss. She knew my history and about all my other jobs. After a few weeks, she asked if I'd like to work full-time with her. It was a pretty decent salary increase, so of course I said 'yes.' At the same time, Glenn, her husband, needed a new secretary at his office, and they offered the job to my mother. Again, it was more money than what she was making as a temp.

"It was great. I could quit my other jobs because I was making more. I was also able to work out and take classes for free, which I really enjoyed. I didn't think I was going to like aerobics, but I discovered the opposite. Because of my interest, Tiffany encouraged me to become an instructor, and I just adored it. I felt like I had figured out what I wanted to do with my life. For the first time since before my father left, I was happy."

She paused, taking a sip of her tea, which had to be cold by now. I waited in silence. While I still didn't understand where the guilt was coming from, it was giving me a glimpse into who Courtney was as a person and what made her tick.

"I knew about Dennis, of course. My mother talked about him, as did Tiffany. I knew he was married, but his marriage was basically over. They weren't divorced, but they were separated. He had moved out of the house, and they were in that space where they were both trying to work out if they wanted to stay together or end it. It was during this time that Tiffany one day asked me if I wouldn't mind teaching her late-afternoon aerobics class, as she was going to a work dinner with Glenn, and there wouldn't be enough time for her to shower and get ready if she taught it. She apologized, saying she had gotten the dates wrong, or she would have planned better.

"Of course I said 'yes.' I would have done nearly anything for Tiffany. I was so grateful for all the help she had given me. She thanked me and then said something about getting Karen, who was one of our personal trainers, to watch the front desk until I could get back after class. Now, Karen was a great personal trainer, but not great at watching the front desk. She loved talking to people and could easily get distracted and not check people in properly, which then created more of a headache for me to fix after the fact. So I said that wouldn't be necessary, as Tiffany wasn't leaving until after class was over. I could just pop out as soon as I was done and cover the desk, so Tiffany could leave.

"I remember how Tiffany got the oddest expression on her face. She said, 'No, Karen can handle it.' I told her it was no trouble, that I didn't mind at all. I'd done it before, and it wasn't a big deal.

"Then she started telling me it would be better if I didn't come out early. In fact, I should stay away until after she left. When I asked her why, she started telling me that Dennis was coming as well, and as this was the first time he was going to one of these dinners single, it would be best to keep things simple for him. Then she went on to talk about how she thought it was a mistake that he'd moved out, and she wished he was bringing Nina, as they really ought to be working on their marriage. She thought it was best that Dennis didn't have any other distractions until he 'got his head on straight and went back to his wife.'

"Well, none of it made any sense to me. I didn't understand how my being at the front desk would have any sort of effect on his relationship with his wife. Then I was hurt, because I thought Tiffany was ashamed of me. I asked Tiffany if that was the case, and she was floored. It was clear she hadn't been thinking that, and she kept assuring me it had nothing to do with me. She just wanted Dennis to do the 'right thing.' Which, again, made no sense to me.

"I couldn't stop thinking about it all day, so of course by the time class was over, I was in the lobby. By that time, I was super curious and wanted to see Dennis for myself.

"I was surprised at how handsome he was. I remember I kind of stood there, uncertain, feeling like I wanted to go back to the ladies' locker room, when he turned. His eyes met mine, and that was it. The attraction was instant, like I had touched a live wire. He came over to introduce himself, and we started talking in the lobby, which is where Tiffany found us after she had finished getting ready.

"I was a little nervous, because it was the first time I didn't do as she asked. My attention was torn between Dennis and watching for her, so I saw her the moment she stepped out of the hallway. Her face went white, and she stopped dead in her tracks. I felt sick. Neither Glenn nor Dennis was paying any attention to her, so they didn't see it, but I knew the truth. It was because I had disobeyed her.

"I rushed up to her, apologizing, telling her I thought she had left. She recovered quickly and gave me this flat smile that didn't reach her eyes before hurrying everyone out of the building. Of course, Dennis wasn't so easily swayed, and a few days later, he showed up at the end of my aerobics class. It was one of Tiffany's days off, so he kept me company for a while as I manned the desk and eventually asked me to dinner. And the rest is history." She hunched over, folding both arms across her belly, as if shielding her baby from the blows of condemnation she was expecting from me.

I, however, was still trying to sort it out in my head. Listening to the story, it seemed to me that Tiffany sensed, correctly, that Dennis would find Courtney attractive and wanted to keep the two from meeting. But Courtney's response still wasn't making sense. I could understand her feeling guilty in the beginning, but once she knew about Dennis's affair with Tiffany, wouldn't she be upset with Tiffany for manipulating her?

"So, I gather Tiffany was pretty upset," I said, when it became clear that Courtney was waiting for me to say something.

Courtney nodded. Her hair had spilled over her face again, so I couldn't read her expression. "Our relationship was never the same after that. I thought it was because she disapproved of my seeing Dennis. He wasn't officially divorced when we started dating, and maybe she thought I was preventing him from getting back together with Nina. But Dennis assured me the marriage was over. It wouldn't have mattered if he had met me or not. And then I thought maybe it was because I disobeyed her ... that she was still angry about that. I apologized, and she said it wasn't a big deal, but I could still tell something was wrong. I asked her a few times to tell me what it was, but she kept insisting that everything was fine ... that it was all in my head. But I knew it wasn't." She paused again. She still hadn't looked up at me, but she was starting to uncurl herself and sit up a little straighter, as if talking about it was finally beginning to free something up inside her.

"So, what happened?" I asked. "Did she fire you, or ...?"

Courtney shook her head. "No, nothing like that. I worked for her until Dennis and I got married, which took a bit as he first needed to finalize the divorce." She smiled at the memory. "Dennis hated waiting. He wanted to marry me right away, but of course, the wheels of justice move at their own pace. Anyway, once we were married, I dropped my schedule back to just teaching classes. We didn't need the money. Dennis made enough for me to stay home, but I liked teaching." She looked away, her eyes full of grief. "Dennis was so good to us. Did you know he even helped out my mother? He found her the cutest little apartment in one of the complexes he owned, so she didn't have to pay rent. Plus, he kept her on his business's health insurance plan, so she was able to drop down to working part-time. He was so caring. He would have made a wonderful father."

"He sounds amazing," I said, but inside, I was struggling to make sense of all the pieces. How could two business partners have completely different financial situations? On one hand, Dennis was supporting both his mother-in-law and his stay-at-home wife, while presumably also paying alimony to the mysterious Nina, whereas Glenn appeared to be unable or unwilling to give his wife a loan for her business.

Perhaps I was being unfair to Glenn, I considered. Perhaps Tiffany was a horrendous business owner, and it made better financial sense to let her sink or swim on her own.

"Anyway," Courtney continued, wiping her eyes with a tissue. "I tried for a long time to fix my relationship with Tiffany. I even asked her to be my maid of honor for my wedding. She declined. Said she was 'too old' for that sort of thing. I tried to talk her into it. I even told her that I owed her for introducing us, but she was pretty adamant. Eventually, I just gave up."

"But you still had to spend time with them, right?" I asked. "I mean, Glenn and Dennis were still business partners. So there were work parties and dinners together?"

"Some," Courtney said. "The work parties weren't really an issue. We could just avoid each other. There were some dinners at each other's houses in the beginning, but they petered out

over time." She stared off into the corner, her expression deject-
ed.

I was completely gobsmacked. Courtney was acting like she
mourned the loss of the relationship with Tiffany—like they had
been best friends until one day they weren't, and Courtney had
no clear reason why. Which made no sense. Tiffany had been
sleeping with Dennis. Why wasn't Courtney furious with her?
For that matter, why hadn't Courtney even brought up the subject? She knew I knew who it was, because her mother had told
me ...

With a sudden, blinding shock, all the pieces swirling around
in my brain clicked into place.

Courtney had no idea who was sleeping with her husband.

Suddenly, it all made sense.

Violet.

She had worked at the firm. Of course she would have seen
Tiffany hanging around. Maybe she even saw Tiffany and Dennis having their affair. And clearly, she never told her daughter
the truth, maybe to save her feelings.

The only thing that didn't make sense was why her mother
hadn't told Courtney before she married Dennis. If Courtney
had known, surely, she would have called off the wedding.

Wouldn't she?

"I don't think you did anything wrong," I said.

Courtney jerked her head up, and for the first time since she
started the story, met my eyes.

"I would have thought it was a strange request, as well,"
I continued. "And if my boss had said that to me, I probably
would have done the same thing ... gone out into the lobby to
take a look at the mystery man myself."

Courtney smiled. "The whole thing was really weird," she
said. "But then, Tiffany hadn't been acting herself for a while.
Honestly, I was wondering if something else was going on,
something with her health. She wasn't focusing the way she
used to. I would catch her sitting at her desk just staring off into
space. And she was more irrational, as well, and making strange

decisions. It was just a weird time. I still wonder if there was something else going on ... something she wasn't telling me."

There absolutely was something else going on that Tiffany wasn't telling her, but it wasn't my place to get into it.

"I did want to ask you, and I get it, if you don't know the answer, but how is Tiffany as a business owner?"

Courtney looked puzzled. "Do you mean was she a good boss? Yes, she was the best."

"No, not just a good boss, although I guess that's part of it. I meant," I hesitated, trying to figure out the right words. "Was she good with numbers? Was Fit for Life profitable? Was she making money?"

Courtney's face cleared. "Oh. I see. Yes, I mean, I think so. I never saw any numbers either way, but the place was always busy, and she was always talking about needing to expand and grow her team. Why do you ask?"

That didn't necessarily mean she was a good businessperson, but it also didn't sound like she was running Fit for Life into the ground. "It's just, when I saw her, I got the distinct impression she was having money issues."

Courtney looked surprised. "This is always the busiest time of year. People come in and buy new memberships for the coming year ... you know, New Year's resolutions and all that. I can't believe she would be having money issues now. There must be some sort of misunderstanding."

"What about Dennis's business?" I pressed. "Do you know if there were any financial issues going on there?"

Her face turned white, which I hadn't expected. I had thought she would deny it like she had about Fit for Life, not stare at me in horror. "Did the police tell you?" she whispered.

I sat up straighter, alarm bells going off in my head. "Tell me what?"

"About the missing money."

"*Missing?*"

Her whole body was trembling. "Yes, and they think Dennis was the one who stole it." She buried her face into her hands, her shoulders heaving.

I sat there, dumbfounded. Dennis stealing money? Was that why he was killed? Because of money?

"*Was* he stealing money?"

She raised her head from her hands, tears streaking down her face. "No!"

"But ..." I gestured around the house. "How was he able to afford all of this plus take care of your mother?"

"The business does well," she insisted. "Dennis would have no need to steal anything! Plus, he told me he had made good investments of his own over the years. That's his job! He's very good at it. Why do you think the business has done so well?"

"So, is Glenn just as successful?" I asked.

"I don't know why he wouldn't be."

I couldn't think of any reason either. I also didn't have any proof he wasn't, except the niggling suspicion that Tiffany's money woes were somehow connected to Glenn—either because she needed an influx of cash and Glenn couldn't or wouldn't give it to her, or because of money problems, she was having to pull more money out of the business than was healthy.

"Did Dennis ever share any worries about the business?"

She rolled her eyes. "He was *always* worried about business. He was always stressed about something. Managing other people's money is stressful. He didn't want to make any mistakes. I didn't ask about particulars. I didn't want him to associate the stress of business with being at home."

If Dennis had been stealing from the business, it seemed pretty clear that Courtney didn't know anything about it. Unless she was a really good actress, which was also possible.

"What about the cops? Are they investigating the missing money?"

Her mouth flattened into a thin line. "I don't know what's going on. I had one cop tell me they only cared about the murder, not the theft. I guess Glenn doesn't want to prosecute since Dennis is dead ... I don't even know if he could."

I looked at her in surprise. "But doesn't Glenn want his money back? How can he do that without there being an investigation?"

"I didn't say there wouldn't be an investigation. I guess Glenn is trying to track it down. He doesn't want any criminal charges. But I don't know, maybe I'm getting it wrong."

I looked at her curiously. "How do you know that?"

"Because Glenn called me," she said.

"He called you?"

She nodded. "After the cops spoke to me. He called me a day later, apologizing for not telling me first. He said he knew I had nothing to do with the theft, and he was trying to work out a way to get it fixed without it hurting me financially, as he knew I had enough to deal with."

"Wow, that was ... pretty generous of him."

Courtney nodded again, her face expressionless. "Glenn was always a little prickly," she said. "A lot of people found him off-putting. But he was always kind to me. I liked him."

I wondered if Glenn's compassion was because he felt a kinship to Courtney because their spouses were having an affair, or if he had a guilty conscience because he was the one who killed her husband. Regardless, if Dennis truly was stealing from the business, that gave both Glenn and Tiffany motive.

"Is there anything else that has come out about Dennis?" I asked.

"What do you mean?"

"Well, any other secrets that might have led to his death."

She gave me a reproachful look. "Isn't that enough?"

Touché, I thought. "What about his affair?" I asked. "Do you know who it was with?"

Her face closed in on itself. "I don't want to talk about it."

Did that mean she knew, or she didn't? "Courtney," I said as quietly and gently as I could. "This is important. If you want me to help, you need to tell me everything you know. Do you know who it is?"

She sat frozen for a moment, and I wondered if she was even going to answer. But finally, she shook her head.

"Then how do you know he was having an affair?"

"Because of the lipstick."

"Lipstick?"

She nodded. "On his shirt collar. It wasn't my shade … not that I would have gotten any on his shirt collar anyway."

"But that doesn't mean he was necessarily having an affair," I said. "He could have hugged someone, maybe a client, who wasn't as careful as she should have been."

"That's what I told myself, too. But then," she paused and swallowed hard. "One of my friends told me she saw him with another woman. She didn't know who, because she couldn't see the other woman's face. But she said they were … were … kissing."

Inwardly, I sighed. I wondered if the friend was actually her mother. I didn't want to push it though, as I had promised Violet that I wouldn't tell Courtney. "I'm sorry, Courtney."

She shrugged—a sad, pathetic movement that didn't do anything to hide the hurt in her eyes. "Doesn't matter now. It's all just water under the bridge."

I couldn't think of anything to say to that.

"I know I keep asking this, but is there anything else I should know about?"

She looked at me, her eyes red-rimmed and hopeless. But there was something else there. Something I couldn't identify.

"I can't think of anything," she said. Her voice matched her eyes. Hopeless and sad.

The more time I spent with her, the more convinced I was that she had nothing to do with her husband's murder.

But that didn't mean I wasn't equally as sure she was still lying to me.

Chapter 11

"I can't believe you went to Courtney's house without me."

I pushed the lemon meringue pie toward Pat. "Have another piece of pie. Did I mention I baked it just for you?" Pat *loved* lemon meringue pie.

She glared at me as she started to cut a second piece. "Don't think I don't know a bribe when I see one," she growled.

"You know I wanted to bring you," I said. "But I also want to get to the bottom of all these secrets."

"And how did that work out for you?" Pat asked, her mouth full of meringue.

I made a face. "Yes, I admit she's still lying. Everyone is still lying. But look at what I *did* discover."

"Dennis is apparently a thief as well as an adulterer," Pat said. "Who could have seen that coming?"

"And the fact that Courtney's mother didn't tell her it was Tiffany," I said. "I'm still struggling to get my head around that."

"I know," Pat said through bites of pie. "I can't imagine not telling Barbara if I knew that the man she was about to marry was also a cheater." Barbara was her daughter.

I picked up my mug. "Was it the money? Was Violet just so exhausted from working so hard all those years, and she thought Dennis would take care of them financially?"

"It's also possible she didn't know," Pat said, licking her fork. "At least, not before the wedding. Maybe Tiffany never came to the office. She did have a business to run, after all. Maybe she and Dennis were more discreet, and Violet only caught them after the wedding."

I took a sip of tea. "That's possible," I said. "That makes more sense, actually, than her knowing and not telling Courtney. She and Courtney seem pretty tight. I don't see a lot of secrets between them."

"You mean besides this one. Violet still isn't telling her about Tiffany."

"Probably because she doesn't want to hurt her," I said.

"So, what's next?" Pat asked.

I sighed. "I'm not sure. I seem to have just as many suspects as when I started, although I will say Glenn has moved closer to the top of the list. He must have been furious at Dennis."

"I'd say it was more likely he hated him," Pat said. "Dennis stole his wife and his money. Wouldn't you hate him?"

I inclined my head. "It might also explain some of Tiffany's reaction," I said. "On one hand, she was quick to accuse Courtney, but the more we talked, the more she seemed to kind of back off from that. Do you think she might suspect her husband?"

Pat pursed her lips. "Maybe. It might not even be conscious. I've found that to be the case more times than not. People know what's going on, but they're too terrified to admit it to themselves."

"Or, what if it was Tiffany, and she's feeling guilty about pinning it on Courtney?" I mused. "What if she did it in a fit of anger? Maybe she and Dennis were having some sort of lover's spat, and then she found out about the money being stolen and just lost it."

"'Poison is a woman's weapon,'" Pat said. "Didn't Agatha Christie say that?"

"Actually, I think that was Sherlock Holmes," I said. "But yes. The choice of sending a poisoned bottle of brandy to the house doesn't fit as well with Glenn. I don't see him wanting to incriminate Courtney, and that scenario definitely makes her the number one suspect. But Tiffany was clearly upset about Courtney marrying Dennis. Maybe she was jealous, because she wanted Dennis, even though she really had no claim on him. Or maybe it was some sort of rivalry. Courtney was younger and prettier, and Tiffany clearly must have known or sensed she was Dennis's type, or she wouldn't have told Courtney not to come out to the lobby in the first place. But whatever it was, she hasn't gotten over Courtney marrying Dennis, so for Tiffany, Courtney being blamed might have been part of the plan."

"You know, if Dennis was stealing from the business, Glenn might not be the only one upset with him," Pat said. "What if he was also stealing from his clients? Maybe one of them found out and got pretty upset."

"That's true." I thought about my meeting with Glenn and how June had interrupted with the announcement of what sounded like an irate client on the phone. Could that client also have been victimized?

"Maybe I need to try harder to get to Nina," I said. "I feel like I still have more questions than answers, and maybe she can help me figure out which direction I should focus on."

"Good idea," Pat said, and pointed a fork at me. "Just make sure you bring me next time. A lemon pie isn't going to save you if you don't."

* * *

I had just finished straightening up the kitchen when the doorbell rang. Assuming it was Pat returning for some reason (perhaps to take home the rest of the pie, which I had urged her to do, but she'd refused, claiming her waistline didn't need the addition of an entire pie in one day). I opened the door expecting to see her standing on the stoop.

Instead, I found Officer Brandon Wyle.

"Well, hello there, officer," I said sweetly. "Is there something I can do for you? Perhaps a custom-blended tea to help with whatever ails you?"

He shot me a look. "I don't think there's a tea out there than can help with what ails me," he said. "May I come in?"

I leaned against the door, even though I knew all my nice, warm air was rushing out. "That depends," I said. "Is this an official or unofficial visit?"

His eyes narrowed. "Unofficial. For now."

"Well, if that's the case, come right in." I held the door open. "I have homemade lemon meringue pie. Would you like a slice?"

"This isn't a social call," he said, stepping inside and removing his jacket.

"Is that a 'yes'?" I asked, heading to the kitchen. Behind me, I heard a sigh.

I had the pie on the table and was making a fresh pot of tea when he appeared in the kitchen. "You don't have to go through any trouble," he said.

"Nonsense," I said, bringing the tea to the table. "I'm happy to provide our law enforcement with refreshment. Now, how can I be of service?"

He sat down but didn't touch the tea or pie. His dark hair was still on the shaggy side—clearly, he hadn't scheduled that haircut yet. His equally dark eyes were hooded as he studied me. "You lied to me."

I widened my eyes. "That's quite an accusation. I hope you have proof to back it up."

"You said you weren't going to investigate Dennis Fallon's murder."

I reached over and started cutting a piece of pie. "Hmmm. I don't recall making that promise."

"We agreed. I said we had it covered, and you didn't need to investigate, and you agreed."

I tilted my head to one side. "Well, that's not how I remember it. I do remember you telling me you had the investigation covered, but as for me agreeing to anything ... I'm pretty certain that didn't happen."

He blew out a frustrated sigh.

I pushed the piece of pie toward him. "Trust me, that pie will make everything better."

He shook his head, but picked up his fork. "Honestly, you're going to be the death of me."

"All I've done is ask a few questions," I said. "No harm in that, and certainly not against the law."

"It is when it's harassment."

My jaw dropped. "Harassment?"

He nodded as he took a bite. "Glenn Haggard wants to file an official complaint. Said you're harassing him and his wife."

I started to laugh. "What? There was no harassment."

"Why don't you tell me what happened and let me be the judge?"

"Well, it's true I spoke to both of them. I made an appointment with Glenn to discuss him becoming my financial advisor. And I met Tiffany because I checked out an aerobics class at Fit for Life. We got to chatting, and she's interested in selling my teas in her business."

There was a pause as Wyle ate and I sipped my tea. Finally, he gestured with his fork. "Continue."

"Well, that's really it."

He raised his eyebrow. "That's it?"

"Well, yeah. Basically. I mean, I'm sure we talked about other things, but that was the gist of the conversation."

"So, you didn't tell either of them that Courtney is your client and then proceed to ask questions about Courtney and Dennis?"

"Oh! Is that what all of this is about?" I shrugged. "Well, I mean, Glenn's business partner just died, so of course it would have been remiss on my part to not ask how his death will impact the business."

Wyle's lips twitched, as if holding back a smile. "And Tiffany? What was the excuse there?"

I took a moment to think about it. "You know, I can't really remember how it came up. I think it was because I was telling her about my appointment with Glenn."

"Why would you tell her that?"

"Well, because they're married." I rolled my eyes. "I thought she might be interested in hearing that I was considering working with her husband."

"How did you know they're married? They don't have the same last name."

"Glenn has a picture of her on his desk," I said. "I noticed it and asked him about it. Anyone having a meeting with him would have done the same."

Wyle shook his head. "I can't believe it."

"What?" My voice was all sweetness and innocence.

He put his fork down and scrubbed his face with his hands. I had the distinct impression he was trying not to laugh. "Okay," he said, removing his hands and sitting back in his chair. "So, officially ..."

"I thought you weren't here officially," I said.

He glared at me. "Officially, you need to leave Glenn alone. Tiffany, too."

"What if I want to hire him to be my financial advisor?"

He gave me another look. I held up my hands in mock surrender. "Okay, okay. I guess he doesn't want my business."

He shook his head again.

"But all kidding aside, is this complaint something I should worry about?"

"Just as long as you leave Glenn and Tiffany alone, there shouldn't be an issue," he said.

"That's it?" I was surprised. "I would have thought there would be more of a ... 'lawyerly' response to such a complaint."

"Well, depending on what was filed, there might have been. But as there is no official complaint, there's nothing to be done."

"But I thought you said Glenn filed a complaint?"

"I said he *wanted* to," Wyle corrected. "Luckily for you, I was the one dealing with him. I was able to talk him out of doing anything official and instead told him I would take care of it."

I wasn't sure if I heard him correctly. "Wait, you were the one who talked him out of filing a complaint against me? Why would you do that?"

He reached for his tea mug. "Honestly? Because I found his complaint ... suspicious."

"Really?" This was getting more and more interesting. "How so?"

"Let me just say that his story and your story were more similar than not," he said drily. "He admitted you had only come to see him once, and that you claimed to be looking for a new financial advisor. It was less clear about why you were seeing his wife, but again, it sounded like you were showing up in her business during business hours. Regardless, I found I was less interested in what you were doing and far more interested that he was upset enough by your questions that he made time in his busy schedule to come down to the station to make a complaint."

"I find that rather interesting myself," I said. I picked up the spatula and gestured to the pie, my actions asking if he wanted another piece. He shook his head.

"So, do you want to tell me what you talked about that got him so hot and bothered?" He flashed a sudden, unexpected grin at me, which caused my stomach to flip inside out. He was really quite good looking when he smiled. Good thing he didn't do it much.

Instead, I dropped my gaze to my tea and thought about what to do. It wasn't like I was under any sort of obligation to not talk to the cops. I wasn't an actual private investigator or anything like that. Nor had I taken any money for what I was doing. But I still felt vaguely uncomfortable, like I might be sharing a confidence that wasn't mine to share.

I decided to start easy, with the things I already knew the cops knew.

"Well, it seems Glenn and Tiffany are having some financial trouble," I said.

"How do you know that?"

"Tiffany made some comments that inferred her business isn't doing well financially," I said. "And Glenn, of course, is saying that Dennis stole money, so my guess is if there are financial issues, he's blaming the theft."

"You don't think that's the case?"

I shrugged. "According to Courtney, he wants to handle the investigation himself. I would think if there was money stolen, he would welcome official help. Wouldn't you?"

Wyle gave me a sideways smile. "We found that interesting, too."

"As for Tiffany, it's clear she's hiding something. I'm not sure what."

"Do you know who Dennis was having the affair with?"

I gave him a look. "I don't know for sure, but it sounds like you've heard the same rumors I have. That it was Tiffany."

He nodded. "It would appear Glenn had motive to kill Dennis. Plus, he would have known about Dennis's cousin."

"I agree. He does look guilty."

Wyle studied me. "But ..."

"I didn't say 'but.'"

He gave me that sideways smile again. "You didn't have to."

"No wonder they pay you the big bucks," I said with my own half-smile before letting it fade. "If Dennis had been killed in some other fashion, maybe a car accident or robbery gone bad, I would absolutely suspect Glenn was behind it somehow. But this? A poisoned bottle of brandy shows up at Dennis's house. Of course Courtney is going to be the prime suspect. Glenn knows this, and if he knows about the affair, he likely sees Courtney as someone who is equally hurt. So why would he want to pin the murder on her?"

"And if he doesn't know about the affair?"

"I still don't see why he would want to hurt Courtney. If he killed Dennis because Dennis was stealing, he knows Courtney would have had nothing to do with it. Again, it makes no sense to pick a murder method that so obviously lays the blame at Courtney's feet."

"On the other hand, he might be thinking if the investigation focuses on Courtney, he'll be less likely to be discovered. Plus, since Courtney didn't do it, maybe he thinks the investigation will clear her."

I snorted. Wyle stared at me.

"Sorry," I said. "I wasn't trying to be skeptical. But the problem with the poison in the bottle as a Christmas gift is that Courtney can't really prove she didn't do it. Glenn seems smarter than that. Unless he thinks it's such a circumstantial case that it will never go to trial. Speaking of circumstantial, have you identified the poison yet?"

I didn't expect Wyle to answer me. But to my surprise, he took out a small notebook and flipped through it. "It's something called 'Aconitum Napellus.'" He pronounced the words slowly.

It took me a few moments to decipher what he said. "Are you talking about Monkshood?"

He stared at me. "Yes. You know what that is?"

"Yes. It's a very dangerous heart and nerve poison. It's an herb that's usually grown only as an ornamental plant because of its dark purple flowers. It's beautiful, but very toxic. In ancient times, they would dip the tips of spears into a poison made of Monkshood before going into battle."

He shut his notebook. "I should have guessed you'd know about it."

"Well, that is what I do," I said modestly. "But now I'm even more convinced it's not Glenn. How would he know about Monkshood?"

"He could research it. You said he was smart."

"Yeah, but he's a numbers guy. I don't see him spending time in the library going through books on herbs. That seems like too much work when there are other ways to kill someone. Although ..." I paused as a thought struck me. "Tiffany is very much into herbs and natural medicine. It's possible she knows about Monkshood."

"So, you think Tiffany did it?"

"Possibly. Or she's got books at home, and Glenn went through them."

Wyle folded his arms across his chest. "So, now you think it's Glenn?"

"He certainly has the motive," I said, although even to myself, I didn't sound convinced.

"So, if you don't think it's Glenn, then who?"

I sighed. "That's the problem. I'm not sure. If not Tiffany or Glenn, then who? Maybe Nina knows."

"The ex?"

I nodded. "I was hoping she would talk to me."

Wyle narrowed his eyes. "Are you going to harass her, too?"

"That wasn't the plan. Of course, it wasn't the plan to harass Tiffany or Glenn, either."

His lips twitched in a faint smile. "If you want to debrief on what you find out, let me know."

I widened my eyes and pressed my hand to my heart. "Does this mean what I think it does? That you're giving me your blessing to investigate?"

Wyle rolled his eyes. "I think 'blessing' is a little strong, but at this point, it seems clear you're going to do what you want, so if you can help solve the case, I'll take it."

"Well, then since you asked so nicely, maybe I will give you a debrief. Although," I frowned, as if mulling it over. "To be honest, I'd rather 'compare notes' than give you a debrief."

His smile widened slightly as he stood up. "Ours wasn't the most helpful of meetings, but maybe you'll have better luck." He waved me back down as I started to stand. "I can see myself out. Thanks for the pie. You're right, it did make everything better." He flashed one last grin as he sauntered out of the kitchen, leaving me to catch my breath.

Brandon Wyle was trouble. No question about that.

I had just finished cleaning up the kitchen a second time when there was another knock at the door. "Grand central station again," I muttered to myself as I went to answer it.

This time, I checked to see who it was before opening the door. There was a man I had never seen before standing on the porch. From what I could tell, he was definitely attractive, with sandy-brown hair and delicate, almost effeminate features, and a bit of a weak chin. I wondered if he was a potential client. I mostly sold to women, but I did have the occasional man stop by.

I opened the door. "Can I help you?"

He raised his head and stared directly into my eyes. His were dark blue and ringed with thick lashes that were wasted on a man. "Are you Charlie Kingsley?"

"I am. And you are ...?"

"Luke." There was something frantic, almost frenzied, about him that made me want to back up a few steps and shut the door. "Luke Zellner. I'm Courtney's lover."

Chapter 12

I watched Luke demolish the rest of the pie. He had been so distraught, I wasn't sure what to do with him other than offer him a cup of tea and dessert, which he accepted. He didn't seem too keen on the tea, but at least I wasn't going to have to worry about any leftover pie.

He was younger than I thought when I saw him standing outside. He was also more muscular—the thin, pale-blue sweater that matched his eyes stretched across his well-developed chest.

"She couldn't have done it," he kept telling me between bites. "Courtney is absolutely the sweetest, most loving person you could ever meet. The fact that anyone thinks she could have done this to anyone, much less her husband, is ludicrous."

I tried not to roll my eyes. Luke had been basically repeating the same thing since he first sat down in my kitchen.

"How long have you two been ... seeing each other?" I winced as the words came out of my mouth. It sounded like I thought there was nothing wrong with what they were doing, when in reality, I was trying to figure out if Courtney's baby was Luke's.

"A few years," Luke said.

I tried to keep the shock from my face, although Luke was looking down at the pie instead of at me anyhow. A few *years*? That would be most of Courtney's marriage. Maybe even before their marriage. Did this mean Dennis had been seeing Tiffany for years, as well? Were Courtney and Dennis even in an actual marriage?

"You've been having an affair for *that* long?" I asked.

Luke stopped chewing and looked at me, his expression slightly sheepish. "Well, no," he admitted. "We've been friends for that long, but it wasn't until this year that things shifted."

"What changed?"

He gave me a surprised look. "What changed? She found out her husband was a lying, cheating bastard, that's what. He doesn't deserve her."

His tone was so angry, I found myself wanting to push my chair back. I wondered if he was angry enough to do something about it.

"So, she started having an affair with you because her husband was having an affair?"

He dropped his fork onto his plate, the contact making a "clinking" noise. "It wasn't like that," he said forcefully, almost as if he were trying to convince himself. "Yes, she was upset, and yes, I was the person she turned to. I was the only one who listened to her. We *were* friends. But sometimes friendships can develop into something more, and that's what happened. That's all it was."

I wondered if Courtney had the same view of their relationship. "How did you two meet?"

His whole body seemed to relax as his lips curled into a smile. "We worked together at Fit for Life," he began.

It was all I could do to keep myself from interrupting with an "Are you kidding me?" How was it that everyone involved in this case seemed to have worked for either Fit for Life or F & H Financial Advisors?

"I'm a personal trainer," he continued, which certainly explained his muscular chest. "And you probably know that Courtney was on staff there, too."

"You weren't?"

He shook his head. "The personal trainers and fitness instructors were all contractors. We just worked when we had clients. Courtney was the exception, although a couple of the personal trainers would also work a few hours a week behind the front desk."

"Does this mean you knew Courtney before she met Dennis?"

He nodded. "We were friends. I was dating someone else before she started going out with Dennis, or I probably would have asked her out sooner. Of course, I thought there was plenty of time. I was such an idiot." He shook his head.

"So, I gather you stayed friends after she got married."

"Yeah. Courtney didn't have a lot of friends to begin with. She had basically worked through her entire teenage years, so she wasn't able to go out and party like other kids her age. But we always got along." He picked up his fork and started playing with what was left of the pie on his plate. "I had to work a lot, too, so I understood."

"And Dennis knew about your relationship?"

He shrugged. "I think so. I was at the wedding. But it wasn't something Courtney and I talked about."

"What did you talk about?"

"Life, I guess." He gave me a lopsided grin. "What do friends talk about?"

"Let me rephrase," I said. "Was she happy? Was she in love with Dennis? Other than the affair, did they seem happy together?"

He took a few moments to answer. "I think, overall, she was content with her life," he said. "Before she got pregnant, she was a little bored, quite honestly. She loved working out—that was another thing we had in common—and she loved teaching aerobics classes, but Tiffany didn't use her as much as she wanted-ed. She told you about the rift between her and Tiffany?"

I nodded.

"Yes, well, because of that, Tiffany didn't schedule her for classes the way she used to, which I know bothered Courtney. Not that she complained. I encouraged her to go to other health and fitness clubs and line up more teaching gigs. It would be easy for her to do, because she's really good. But for a long time, she resisted."

"Do you know why?"

Luke scooped up a bite of pie and popped it into his mouth. "I think because she didn't want to hurt Tiffany," he said. "I think a part of her really thought Tiffany would eventually come around and want to be friends again, but if Courtney was working for the competition, that would be it. Of course, that didn't happen. I think Courtney had just about decided to shop her talents around when she got pregnant, which of course scuttled those plans."

"Speaking of the baby," I said, grateful he'd brought it up, as I had been trying to figure out how to weave it into the conversation. "Do you know if ..." my voice trailed off as I realized just how nosy I sounded.

"If it's mine, you mean?" He shook his head as he went back to staring at his plate. "It's not. But I wish it was," he muttered into the pie.

I had to wonder about his motives. How much did he *really* wish the baby was his? Enough to send Dennis a surprise gift on Christmas Eve?

"This has been really helpful, Luke," I said with a smile. "But I am curious. Why are you here?"

He stopped eating, his fork still in the air, to stare at me. "What do you mean? Aren't you helping Courtney figure out who killed Dennis?"

I nodded. "I'm trying. Did she tell you to come talk to me?"

"No. She doesn't know I'm here."

"Then how did you know I'm helping her?"

He shot me a look. "Are you serious? This is Redemption. Word gets around."

I supposed it would, especially with Glenn trying to lodge a complaint about me. I could still remember how fast word had spread about my tea business. Still, it left me feeling a bit uneasy. I wasn't keen on starting a detective business.

"So, what did you come to tell me? Just that she couldn't have done it?"

Luke scraped off the last piece of pie. "No. Well, yes, it's true that she couldn't have done it, but mostly, I wanted to tell you who did."

I sat up a little straighter. "You know that? Who is it?"

"A client."

It was all I could do not to roll my eyes. "A client? That's really vague. Any idea which one?"

"Probably one involved in Maple Leaf Grove."

"What's that?"

He gave me a surprised look. "You don't know? It was an investment project F & H was a part of that ended up a complete disaster. You didn't hear about it?"

I shook my head.

Luke settled back in his chair, like he was getting ready to share a story. "Well, one of my clients was involved, which was how I found out about it."

"One of your personal-training clients?" I was trying to figure out how investing and working out went together.

"No, one of my handyman jobs." He saw the confusion on my face and clarified. "I do a lot of odd jobs. Handyman, construction, personal training. Altogether, it's a living. Anyway, Mr. Oldman is a long-time client. I've been helping him out for years. I basically have a standing appointment one afternoon a week to do whatever needs to be done around his house or yard. He's a great guy. Pays me for a full day's work even though I'm usually only there half the day, and I rarely work the whole time then. He always wants me to stay and chat for a while. He was the one who told me about Maple Leaf Grove, because he was an investor and thought maybe I could get some steady work there."

"Well, what is it?" I asked again, trying to hide my impatience.

He picked up his tea and took a sip, making a slight face. "It was supposed to be a brand-new, high-end subdivision outside of Riverview. You know how much that city is growing, right? It's just taking off. Anyway, I'm not sure of all the specifics—you could talk to Mr. Oldman about it if you wanted—but F & H was one of the main investors, along with a bunch of their clients, like Mr. Oldman. The land was purchased, and it was gorgeous. Just a perfect site for a beautiful neighborhood. Plans had been drawn up, contractors were hired, work got started, and then the EPA stepped in and designated it a 'superfund site.' The investors lost hundreds of thousands of dollars."

My eyes widened. "A superfund site? You mean, one of those plots of land that was once home to an old gas station, and the gas tank leaked?"

He nodded solemnly. "Yes, except this was an old chemical waste site, so it was even worse. Apparently, it all happened back in the twenties. The company basically just covered everything with dirt, and after a few years, sold it. I think it was sold a couple other times before it was set to become part of the new Maple Leaf Grove subdivision."

I pressed my hand to my mouth. "Oh no."

"Superfund sites" were called that because some sort of environmental damage had been done—like a leaking underground gas tank—and before you could do anything with the property, like build or develop it, you would have to clean it up. It was incredibly expensive, which is why the EPA had set up a superfund account to help pay for it. The problem was that, even with superfund money, it was too cost prohibitive. So, the properties tended to just sit there, abandoned and forlorn, wasting away.

"I don't understand," I said. "How did they not know? Didn't they do their due diligence?"

Luke shrugged. "That's the question of the hour. How did it get so far in the process without someone, somewhere, realizing what was happening? Why weren't the proper tests done before the sale? Everyone is pointing fingers at everyone else, and as there were multiple entities involved in the deal, it's not clear who was actually in charge."

"What about who sold them the land? Couldn't the investors go back to them and at least get their money back?"

"They're in the process of trying," Luke said. "There are attorneys involved, and lawsuits, but apparently, the company that sold it is claiming they didn't know, and I guess it's a pretty convincing case. So, it's not good."

"Wow. So, F & H was a part of the whole thing?"

"The investment part. They were the ones lining up the investors, so as you can imagine, the other investors are pretty upset."

I wondered if this was what the man who had called Glenn's office the day I was there was upset about. I couldn't think of his name … something German, I thought. But if he was one of the investors, it made sense why he would be agitated, and why Glenn clearly didn't want to take the call. "I agree this all sounds pretty bad, and Glenn really has his hands full right now, dealing with it alongside Dennis's death. But, speaking of Dennis, how does this tie into his murder? I get that the investors would be upset with him, but there's probably a lot of people involved in that debacle for them to be upset with. And as far as I know, Dennis is the only one who is dead."

Luke leaned forward slightly, as if we were in the middle of Aunt May's diner rather than my kitchen, and he didn't want anyone overhearing him. "Well, rumor has it that even though Dennis had brought it up with his clients, he hadn't invested all that much of his own money."

"Really?" That was a bit surprising. "Does anyone know why?"

"Dennis claimed it was because he had money invested in other projects and wasn't liquid enough to put all that much into this one."

"That sounds reasonable," I said, thinking about what Courtney had said about her husband's successful investments. "Did the investors not believe him?"

"Not really. Some of them, like Mr. Oldman, didn't think it was intentional, but rather that he handled things wrong."

I frowned. "Intentional? People really thought Dennis was trying to scam the investors on purpose?"

Luke nodded. "A few did. They thought Dennis knew exactly what was going on and still sold them the opportunity. But I think most of them were of the same mind as Mr. Oldman, which was that Dennis had a feeling something was off and therefore was cautious with his own money. But if that's true, he also shouldn't have sold it to everyone else."

"But why would Dennis sell something that he knew was a bad investment?" I asked. "Was he just a bad person?"

"I don't think that was it," Luke said. "I never got that sense of him. But, yeah, the lack of a motive as to why he would be involved on any level, including tainting his business by association, is why I think most people just figured he was guilty of terrible judgement."

I paused, turning over the new pieces of information in my mind. "The ones who thought Dennis knew," I said slowly. "I take it there's been no recourse? They just think Dennis screwed them, and there's no way to get their money back?"

"Yep," Luke said. "Which is why I think one of them killed him. Not because he thought he'd get his money back, but just because he wanted Dennis to pay."

The more I thought about it, the more it made sense. "What about Glenn?"

"Oh, Glenn," Luke let out a sigh. "He definitely invested a lot. Maybe a little too much. No one thinks he had anything to do with it."

Well, that explained Glenn and Tiffany's financial predicament. If Glenn had lost a ton of money in Maple Leaf Grove on top of Dennis stealing from the business, no wonder things were tight. Add to the fact that F & H had probably lost clients due to this whole fiasco, and Tiffany taking on janitorial duties made sense. It was entirely possible that she was supporting them financially, at this point.

It also moved Glenn to the top of the suspect list again. How angry and resentful must he have been at Dennis?

Enough to kill him?

"Whoever killed him also wouldn't care if Courtney was the one who was blamed," Luke interrupted my thoughts. Flattening his mouth, he continued, "No, they wouldn't care at all."

"Did you tell the police about this?"

He looked away. "Not yet. I know they really zeroed in on Courtney, and if they realize we are involved ..." He raised his hands, palms up.

"Yeah, I can see that." Cleary, if the cops knew Courtney was also having an affair, all that would do is strengthen their case against her. "Do you have the names of the investors who were the most upset?"

"Right here," he said, digging into his jeans pocket. He pulled out a crumpled piece of paper and handed it over to me.

I smoothed out the wrinkles and studied the three names on the list. Walt Barr, Jim Hacker, and Ned Ardelt. None of them rang any bells.

"I gave you their phone numbers, too, as well as Mr. Oldman's contact information in case you want to talk to him," Luke said.

"I see that," I said. "So, I take it it's okay if I call all of them?"

Luke nodded, his eyes bright and eager to please. "My phone number is on there, too. If you need any help. Or anything."

I folded the paper up. "I definitely will."

Chapter 13

"I met Luke," I said.

There was silence on the other end of the phone.

"Courtney? Are you still there?"

The sound of throat-clearing. "I'm still here," she said in a small, quiet voice.

"Luke said you two were having an affair. Is that true?"

More silence.

"Courtney?"

I was about to hang up and drive over to her house to confront her in person when she started to talk. "It was a mistake," she said, her voice still low.

I closed my eyes. "Courtney, I thought you said you were going to be honest with me?"

"I am!"

"Not telling me about an affair you're having is not being honest with me."

"Had, not having," she corrected, her voice forceful. There was a muffled dragging sound on her end, like she was pulling out a kitchen chair to sit down. "Look," she said, her voice so quiet, I had to strain to hear her. "It was one time, and it was nearly a year ago. I had just been told about Dennis kissing another woman, and I was a wreck. Luke met up with me after I taught my class. We went out for coffee, I told him everything, and … well, one thing led to another."

"Is the child you're carrying Luke's?"

"No!" The answer was immediate and firm. "It was that one time, nearly a year ago. I knew right away I had made a huge mistake, and I told him we could never do it again. He agreed, although I could tell he was disappointed. We still hung out, but nothing else happened."

"You're sure?"

"Yes, I'm sure. I'm telling you the truth." She sounded like she was close to tears. "I know you may not believe this, but I love ... loved my husband. I wanted to make my marriage work. I was devastated when I found out about the cheating and, well, I didn't handle it well. But that mistake woke me up. I got my head on straight and started focusing on making my marriage work."

"Then why didn't you ever tell Dennis you knew he was having an affair?" I half expected her not to answer, as it was really none of my business. But I was also sick of having information withheld from me. I was trying to do Courtney a favor, yet obstacles kept getting tossed in my path at every turn.

She hesitated. "It's hard to explain."

"Why don't you try?"

"Because ... I guess I kind of felt like if he said it, that he was having an affair, it would make it real. And if it became real, then there was the possibility he would leave me for her. So, I guess ... I thought if we didn't talk about it, if instead I just focused on being the best wife I could be, he would ... well, forget about her and stay with me."

There was so much I wanted to say. How trying to build a relationship on a lie never works. That hiding from the truth never worked out for anyone, because the truth always comes out in the end. But what was the point? Dennis was gone. And it wasn't like she had asked for my help with her relationships.

Still, my heart hurt for her. She was so young and already had a lot of strikes against her. I wondered if she would ever be able to move past her trauma and wounds and find the relationship she clearly craved.

For not only her sake, but for that of her baby, I truly hoped she would.

"Do you know about Maple Leaf Grove?"

"Oh no," she said.

I took that as a "yes."

"Why 'oh no'?"

"Because it wasn't his fault!" Her voice was a plaintive cry.

"What wasn't his fault?"

"The project! I know what people are saying, but it wasn't his fault. It wasn't even his idea."

"Courtney, slow down," I said. "Start from the beginning. Are you saying that it was Glenn's idea to invest in Maple Leaf Grove?"

"Yes! That's exactly it." Her voice still had an edge of hysteria to it, but I could tell she was trying to calm herself. "Dennis always had a bad feeling about that project. From the very beginning. But Glenn was so excited about it. He thought it was going to be their big break ... put their business on the map, maybe even get them bigger clients out of Milwaukee or even Chicago. Dennis wasn't as convinced." She sighed. "He didn't want to put any money into it, but felt like he had to, mostly to support Glenn. So he purposefully only put a small amount in. If we lost it, we lost it—it wasn't going to hurt us one way or another, and if the project was as successful as Glenn kept saying, well, that would be okay, too. He would admit he was wrong and be fine with the small return. He told me over and over he hoped he WAS wrong. He didn't want to see anyone lose their shirt over this, but unfortunately, he was right."

"If he was so hesitant about Maple Leaf Grove, why did he sell it to his clients?"

"He didn't," Courtney said firmly. "Glenn was selling it. Not Dennis."

"Then why is everyone blaming him?"

"That's the problem. I don't know," she wailed. "I don't understand what's going on. Why does everyone think Dennis was the reason they lost their money? Or why do they think he stole money from F & H? He was a good, honest man. I don't know why they're saying things like this about him."

"Do you have any idea who was to blame?" I asked. "Who else would have been stealing from F & H, if not Dennis?"

"I don't know," Courtney said. "They have a secretary; I can't remember her name right now. There's also a bookkeeper and a couple of junior associates ... someone named Rick, I think? Or maybe Dick. I can't remember." She sighed. "I'm not that much help, I know. I didn't know any of them very well, but I can't imagine anyone stealing money from anyone. I keep thinking it's some sort of mistake."

"We can only hope," I said, although I was starting to wonder if Courtney was for real. Could she possibly be that innocent, or was it all an act?

And, if it was all an act, did that mean I was on a wild goose chase, and Courtney was guilty after all?

"I have to ask," I continued, even though I knew I was sounding like a broken record. "Why didn't you tell me about Maple Leaf Grove?"

"Why would I tell you?" she asked, sounding genuinely bewildered. "What does Maple Leaf have to do with Dennis's death?"

I closed my eyes, willing myself to be patient. "Luke was the one who told me, because he thought one of the investors in Maple Leaf might be responsible for Dennis's death."

"What?" Courtney sounded shocked. "No. No, that can't be. Dennis's clients are good people. They wouldn't do something like that."

"It *is* possible," I said. "Both you and Luke are telling me that people were pretty angry at Dennis. Rightly or wrongly, it sounds like they were blaming him."

"But, to kill him? That seems extreme."

"I agree. But people kill people over money all the time."

"But it's not like they'd get their money back if Dennis died."

"Courtney," I was trying really hard not to sound as impatient as I felt. "Who do you think killed Dennis?"

"I don't know," she said. "That's why you're helping me look into it."

"Yes, but you do understand it's likely going to be someone you know, right?"

"But ... no. There must be a mistake," she fretted. "An accident."

"And what if there isn't?" I asked. "What if whoever did it truly intended on killing Dennis?" I didn't really like pushing her. I knew she was still grieving and pregnant, but I also felt that, if she continued to close her eyes to reality, things were going to get a lot worse for her.

"Then it must be someone I don't know," she said. "A stranger."

"How would a stranger know Dennis's favorite brandy? Or about his cousin?"

"Well, maybe Dennis told someone, and someone else overheard?" she guessed. "You know, some sociopath."

"Seriously," I said. "You're going with that?"

"There has to be some explanation."

"There *is* an explanation," I said. "And that explanation is simple—someone you know killed your husband."

"But ... but that would mean I know someone who is capable of doing something like that," she burst out. "And that can't be. It just can't."

"Why not?"

"Because I should be able to sense it!" She was completely distraught. "I should have known. Just like I should have known my father was about to leave us. I caught him as he was packing. I asked him why he was packing, and he said he wasn't ... that he was just packing a bag to donate to Goodwill and would be right back. And I *believed* him. I really thought he was coming right home. I didn't sense anything. And now, you're telling me someone I know killed my husband, and I didn't sense that evil, either? How could I be such a lousy judge of character? What is *wrong* with me?"

I stayed silent, listening to Courtney's hitching breath. It sounded like she was crying. "Courtney," I said very quietly. "It's not your fault your father left you."

"But I should have *known*. Other people know when things are off. Why don't I?"

"Sometimes people know, but a lot of times, they don't," I said reassuringly. "People are blindsided all the time by the actions of others. You wanted to believe your dad. There's nothing wrong with that. And it certainly doesn't mean you're a lousy judge of character."

"But my dad wasn't the only one," Courtney said, her breath hitching again as she tried to control her tears. "Dennis cheated on me, and I didn't know it. And what if ... what if he really *did* steal that money? How could I not have known?"

"Half the spouses in this country are cheating, and most of the time, their partners don't know," I said. "It doesn't mean anything. As for what Dennis did or didn't do, let's just wait and see what happens. Maybe it is all a mistake like you said. Okay?"

"Okay," she said, her voice small.

"Is there *anything* else you should tell me? Even if it doesn't seem like it has anything to do with Dennis's death?"

She paused for a moment. "I don't think so," she said, seeming a little uncertain. Then, more firmly. "No, no, I don't think so."

I wasn't sure if I believed her, but that would have to do.

***

"*Courtney* is having an affair, too?" Pat's mouth was open, forming a round O, her expression incredulous. "Are you kidding me?"

"I know," I said, depositing a plate of pumpkin bread in the middle of the table. "It's like every time I turn around, I discover yet another pin dropping."

Pat eyed the plate of bread. "Any more pie?" she asked hopefully.

I shook my head regretfully. "'Fraid not. Wyle and Luke finished it off."

"You should have hidden the leftovers," she grumbled.

I nudged the bread closer. "Pumpkin bread is very festive this time of year. Very soon, there will be no more pumpkin bread—or pumpkin anything—until next fall. So enjoy it."

Pat muttered something under her breath but took a slice. "You know, I do remember hearing about that Maple Leaf fiasco. Richard has a coworker who invested. He had tried to talk Richard into it, too, but Richard wasn't interested. He's not a big on risk-taking. He prefers putting money in savings accounts and US bonds. Needless to say, when it fell apart last summer, his coworker didn't say too much about it."

"Can you ask Richard if his coworker thinks Dennis was to blame?"

Pat frowned as she popped a piece of pumpkin bread into her mouth. "I can ask. I don't know if we'll get the answer, though. The guy is pretty touchy on the subject, mostly because for a while, you couldn't shut him up about it. He was trying to get the entire office to join him. I think one or two did, but he was so obnoxious about it, it turned a lot of people off. But let me see what I can find out. What about the names Luke gave you? Were any of them helpful?"

"They were certainly angry," I said as I twirled my mug around. I had spent the evening after Luke left on the phone, mostly getting yelled at. "Walt was especially furious. The moment I brought up Dennis, he ranted and raved. He even said he wasn't sorry he was dead."

Pat's eyebrows went up. "Really?"

"Yeah." I continued to twirl my mug, remembering how I had to hold the phone away from my ear as I listened to Walt. "He's also pretty convinced that Dennis was stealing from F & H. He's sure Dennis was a shyster, and the world is better off without him in it."

"Do you think Walt could have killed Dennis?"

"It's possible," I said. "I was going to ask him if he knew what Monkshood is, but then I thought it might be better coming from the police. If Walt is the killer, I didn't want to tip my hand."

Pat nodded. "That makes sense."

"I took notes," I said, grabbing a notebook from the counter to show her.

"You're going to give that to Wyle?"

"A copy," I corrected. "But yes. If he's not talking to the Maple Leaf investors, he really should."

"Are you going to tell Wyle about Luke?"

I closed the notebook and placed it next to my tea. "I don't know yet," I said. "I mean, I should. Luke definitely has motive, as he's clearly in love with Courtney. Although that gives Courtney even more motive than she had before. I feel like I should share it, but I don't know."

Pat cocked her head as she studied me. "You don't think Luke did it?"

I sighed. "Not particularly. He didn't *feel* like a killer. You know what I mean?"

Pat gave me a look. "Because you know what a killer feels like, right?"

"Ha," I said, smiling like I was in on the joke as I picked up my tea, if only to give myself a reason to look down and hide my eyes. As good a friend as Pat was, she didn't know all my secrets. She especially didn't know that I actually had quite a lot of experience on the subject of killers.

"But seriously, he had this puppy-dog energy about him. So eager to please. I suppose anything is possible, but Walt felt like a much better lead. Although I don't know if Walt would be all that into poisoning. He seems more like a 'shoot 'em in the parking lot' type of fellow."

"Yeah, the method is the stickler," Pat mused. "There certainly seems to be enough people who were angry enough at Dennis to wish him dead. But to be calculated enough to set up sending him a poisoned bottle of brandy as a pretend gift from his cousin seems a little ... cold-blooded."

"That's where I always get stuck," I said. "Figuring out who has the motive and would pick that specific method. Monkshood, of all things."

"Where would you even find Monkshood?" Pat asked. "Especially now. It's not like it's growing in anyone's backyard."

"Some herbalists sell it," I said. "There are those who claim the herb has some therapeutic uses."

"I thought you said it was quite toxic."

"It is," I said. "I wouldn't use it for anything. But some do. Especially in Chinese medicines. Apparently, it's good for relieving pain, and it also may help with some cardiac problems."

"Really? So you can buy it here?"

I nodded. "The problem is that it's very easy to overdose. It doesn't take much for Monkshood to become toxic. There are other, less lethal ways to help with pain than Monkshood. At least, that's my opinion."

Pat shook her head. "Wow. I had no idea."

"That's the thing. It's not like it's that obvious of a poison to use. The obvious choice would be to get some rat poison. It's easy to get your hands on, and everyone knows it's lethal. But Monkshood? Maybe I'm overthinking things, but right now, all the pieces aren't fitting together. I don't know if I'm missing a couple of crucial ones, or if I'm not looking at what I have in the right way yet."

Pat gave me a sympathetic look. "Well, maybe Wyle can shed some light on this when you give him your notes. When are you going to do it?"

"After I talk to Nina." I grinned at her. "I told him I'd share any insights with him."

Pat stared. "You're talking to Nina?"

"I am," I said, as I stood up. "And so are you. Come on, she's expecting us."

"Seriously? And you couldn't have said something sooner?" Pat glared at me as she finished off the last of the pumpkin bread. "It's a good thing you're such a good cook. Otherwise, we would definitely have issues."

Chapter 14

"So, Charlie," Nina said as she handed me a delicate, white porcelain cup rimmed with gold. "You're the one who makes teas, correct?"

"I am indeed," I said, accepting the cup.

"I've been meaning to call you for a while," she said, giving me a faint smile. "I've been hearing rave reviews."

"It's wonderful," Pat chimed in beside me. "Highly recommend. Best tea you'll ever have."

"Well, then, I definitely feel I should apologize in advance for what I'm serving you. It's store-bought."

"I'm sure it will be fine," I lied. Inwardly, I was kicking myself. I should have brought some samples with me.

Nina gave me another thin smile as she handed a cup to Pat. She was about as opposite of Courtney as one could be. Tall and rawboned, while Courtney was petite and curvy, although the pregnancy certainly added to the curves. Courtney's face was heart-shaped, while Nina's was long, thin, and narrow, with high cheekbones and deep-set, dark-brown eyes. Her brown hair was cut short in a no-nonsense style, which her clothes matched—a dark-blue blazer with a white blouse and black trousers. She would never be called "pretty" or "cute," but she was imposing, and at one time, maybe even striking.

Her house was decorated in a similar no-nonsense manner—navy-blue carpet, beige couch and matching chairs, oak coffee table and bookshelf, and red and blue accents. It was all very neat and sterile.

Nina seated herself in one of the beige chairs and crossed her legs. "Before we get started, I feel like I should warn you that if you're here to talk about Dennis's murder, I'm afraid I'm not going to be of much help. I haven't spoken to Dennis in, oh, at least two years. So, I really don't know anything."

"I'm more interested in learning more about Dennis the person," I said.

Nina's eyebrows raised as she took a sip of tea. "Oh?"

"Yes, I'm hearing a lot of contradictory information about him, and I thought maybe you could fill in some details."

Nina pursed her lips. "I can certainly try."

"So, what was Dennis like?"

"Like?"

"Back when you were married to him," I said. "How would you describe him?"

Nina sat back slightly in her chair. "Dennis was one of those men who could walk into a room and own it," she said. "It's what made him such a good salesman. When he was speaking to you, you felt like the only person in the world. It was truly a gift."

"How did you two meet?"

"Back in college." She paused, her face softening and a smile playing on her lips, and suddenly, I could see the echoes of the beauty she once was. Lacking typical generic prettiness, Nina's looks would have once been unique and noteworthy. "I thought he was such an arrogant jerk. I wanted nothing to do with him. In retrospect, I don't think he was used to anyone saying 'no' to him, which probably really piqued his interest. He asked me out sixteen times before I said 'yes.' For two months, he would wait outside my English Lit class to ask me out again. Finally, I asked what it would take to get him to leave me alone. He said I had to agree to go out with him one time. So, against my better judgement, I did." She shook her head. "The rest is all history."

"How long were you two married?"

"Legally, we were married almost twelve years, but the marriage died way before the legal end."

"Why did it end?"

She sighed. "Because I finally realized I was done sharing him. I wanted a real marriage, not one where I was always in second place."

My eyes widened. Was she talking about Tiffany? "Who were you sharing him with?"

"His work," she said, with more vehemence than I would have expected from someone who had been divorced for several years. "I finally woke up one morning and realized the reason why I was so unhappy was because all along, he had been married to his business, not me. I asked him to move out, said I wanted a trial separation. I thought that might wake him up, but instead, it seemed to put us on a path that ultimately ended in divorce."

While this was certainly consistent with what Courtney said about Dennis working all the time, I wondered if it was the full story. "It was only his work that was the problem?"

Nina lifted an eyebrow. "What else? Or are you asking if he was cheating on me?"

"It's come up that Dennis might not have been completely faithful."

Her smile was sad. "If you're implying that Courtney stole him away, as much as I despise her, it isn't true. We were already legally separated and headed for divorce when Dennis met her. Her being in the picture didn't change a thing."

I wondered about the despising comment, but decided to come back to it. "No, actually it's Tiffany I'm wondering about."

Nina's eyes widened. "*Tiffany*?" She burst out laughing. "Oh heaven's, no. He wouldn't have an affair with Tiffany."

Pat and I glanced at each other. "How can you be so sure?"

Nina put her tea down on the table and picked up a napkin to dab at the corners of her eyes. "Because I was there at the beginning. Who told you this nonsense? Was it Tiffany?"

I had a feeling that bringing up Courtney's mother wouldn't be the right move. "It was actually someone who saw them together."

Nina made a face. "What did they see? Them kissing?" She rolled her eyes. "Tiffany has been after Dennis since they first met. Dennis was never even remotely interested in her."

"But ..." I hesitated, glancing again at Pat, who looked as surprised as I. "If they were kissing ..."

"It meant nothing," she said firmly. "It was likely instigated by Tiffany, but whatever that person saw, I can assure you, it wasn't what it looked like."

"How can you be so sure?"

Nina sighed and recrossed her legs. "I take it no one told you how it all started. So, Dennis and Glenn met in college. They were roommates. I'm not sure how Glenn met Tiffany ... I think at a party, maybe ... but they were dating off and on when he brought her to this tailgating party. Dennis and I were both there; we were on our third date, and I still wasn't sure about him. Tiffany took one look at him, and that was it. She was hooked. It was written all over her face.

"Needless to say, Dennis didn't feel the same way. He was cordial and friendly toward her, but that was it. Our relationship was one of those on-again, off-again types back then, and unfortunately for Tiffany, I think she read into that the wrong way. I think she thought Dennis and I were going to break up, and once we did, she would swoop in and get him. But for her to know if that happened, she had to stay in the know. So, she kept dating Glenn.

"Anyway, as you've probably guessed, that didn't happen. It took a couple of years, but eventually, our relationship turned serious, and Dennis and I got engaged. Shortly after that, Glenn asked Tiffany, and she agreed." Nina shook her head. "For the life of me, I don't know why. It was clear she didn't love him. Why Glenn asked her and why she accepted is a mystery. My suspicion is that Glenn didn't have much experience with women, and he didn't think he could do much better than Tiffany. As for Tiffany," Nina shrugged. "Maybe she thought it was her way of staying in Dennis's life ... like one day, he would look up and see her and realize what he had been missing. Or maybe because she had already devoted so much time to being in a relationship with Glenn, she didn't want to admit defeat. But, whatever the reason, about three months after we were married, they tied the knot."

"Still," I said. "Something could have changed. Maybe after you two separated, he started to see Tiffany in a different light."

Nina made a face. "I highly doubt it. First off, Dennis had enough trouble balancing his business and a relationship, much less trying to squeeze in an affair. And second, I can't see him doing that to Glenn."

It was clear nothing I could say was going to convince Nina. I studied her as she sat in the chair, cool and unruffled. Was it possible that Courtney and Violet were both wrong? That Dennis wasn't having an affair? I decided to switch gears. "What was his relationship with Glenn like?"

Nina reached for her tea. "It was a case of opposites attract. And I mean *polar* opposites. Dennis had all the charm and charisma, while Glenn was more on the numbers and analytics side. As far as I could tell, they continued to get along well even when they were business partners. I know that friendships can sometimes fall apart in those situations, but that doesn't seem to be the case with Dennis and Glenn. Dennis would never hear or say a word against Glenn."

I cocked my head. Another odd turn of phrase from Nina. "What was your relationship like with Glenn?"

Nina looked faintly surprised. "How is that relevant? I haven't talked to any of them in years."

I smiled. "Simple curiosity. I'm also just wondering how you would know that Dennis would never say a word against Glenn."

Nin's lips curled up. "Well, to be quite frank, I warned Dennis not to start a business with Glenn."

"Why?"

"I never trusted him. There was something about him. Something ... slippery. Dennis told me it was all in my head."

"Have you heard about Maple Leaf Grove?"

Nina pressed her lips together and shook her head. "A terrible investment. I don't know who was in charge over there or how the necessary testing wasn't completed before the sale."

"Did you know people are saying that it was Dennis's fault?"

"Dennis?" Nina laughed again, but it wasn't quite as hard as before. "That's ridiculous. What proof do they have?"

"That he didn't put enough of his own money in," I said. "He barely invested anything."

"Well of course he didn't. Dennis knows a good investment when he sees one, and he also knows a bad investment. It's like he can smell them. It was why he was so good at his business."

"So you don't think it was Dennis's doing?"

"If anyone was to blame, it would be Glenn," Nina said firmly. "Glenn always had a weakness for get-rich-quick investments. I can't tell you how often Dennis talked Glenn out of one hairbrained scheme or another. Maple Leaf Grove has Glenn's fingerprints all over it."

"Glenn is also saying that Dennis was stealing from the business."

"*What*?" In her shock, Nina spilled her tea onto her lap. Pat reached over to hand her a napkin. "That's even more preposterous than Dennis being in charge of Maple Leaf Grove."

"So, you don't think he was stealing money, then."

"If anyone is stealing money from that business, it's Glenn," Nina said as she furiously scrubbed her pants with the napkin.

Pat and I looked at each other. *Glenn*?

"But, if that were the case, why would Glenn even bring it up?" I asked. "Dennis is gone. So why would he even talk about it?"

"Probably because someone figured it out, and now, he's trying to save his bacon. Glenn never did anything unless there was a clear benefit to him." Nina stopped her scrubbing and eyed both of us. "Look, I know I was married to the man, so maybe you think I'm biased, but it's not even possible that Dennis *could* be stealing. He was the salesman, remember? Glenn was the one who was in charge of the bookkeeping and numbers."

"I thought Courtney said they had a bookkeeper."

"So what if they did?" Nina said impatiently. "I said Glenn was in charge, not the one necessarily doing the work. He's the CFO, so if anyone could cook the books, he could."

I was starting to get a very bad feeling about the whole thing. "If what you're saying it true, do you think Glenn is capable of killing Dennis to hide all the lying and stealing he was doing?"

Nina looked me directly in the eye. "Absolutely."

Chapter 15

As we were leaving, I asked Nina about what she'd said about Courtney. "You said you despised her," I said. "I'm just curious as to why. Do you think she might have had anything to do with Dennis's death?"

Nina let out a short bark of laughter. "Oh, heaven's no. It's ... well, it's a little hard to explain."

I was by the front door, about to open it, but I stopped and turned around. The hesitancy in Nina's voice was like nothing I had heard from her throughout the entire interview.

She stood there biting her lip. "She's just so ... submissive. Her entire life revolved around Dennis. I never could stand women like that. All my life, they irritated me. 'Have a life,' I would think to myself. 'A man doesn't define you—only you can do that.'" She paused and gave me a twisted smile. "I knew the moment I met her that Dennis would adore her. A big reason why our relationship wasn't working was because we both had completely different careers and focuses, and he really needed a woman who would be there for him. She was exactly right for that." Her smile turned sad. "Maybe I despise her because she was able to give him what I never could."

"You were married a long time," I said quietly. "It sounds like he really tried to make it work. Clearly, he did love you."

"Unfortunately, despite what they say in romance novels, love isn't always enough."

I had no good answer for that, so instead, I thanked her for her time and squeezed her hand. I could write a book on how love isn't always enough.

"That was something," Pat said after we stepped outside, the door closed firmly behind us. "Are we back on the Glenn-did-it train?"

"Maybe," I said. "Nina was certainly compelling." I glanced over my shoulder at the neat and tidy ranch house and could have sworn I saw a curtain fall, as if Nina had moved to the window to watch us go. "But I think we need more."

Pat turned to me, an eyebrow quirked up. "More? As in more evidence? How are we going to get that?"

We reached the car, and I went over to unlock Pat's door before moving to my side. I waited until we were both settled inside before I answered. "If what Nina said is true, it's possible Dennis suspected something was wrong in the business. According to Courtney, Dennis seemed more upset and preoccupied with work than usual these past six months or so. That could be why."

"It's also when Maple Leaf was falling apart," Pat said. "That would certainly cause a lot of stress."

I frowned. "Possibly. It would cause stress, yes. But I don't know. Courtney made it seem like he was bringing more work home than usual. What work would he have with Maple Leaf? It doesn't sound like he had that much to do with it at all."

"Maybe he was trying to save the business by finding more investments."

'Maybe. Or maybe he was starting to suspect Glenn."

"Okay, so what if you're right?" Pat asked. "Where are we going to look for evidence? It's not like we can search Dennis's office at F & H. Even if Glenn didn't call the cops the moment he saw you, he's not just going to let us stroll in there and start digging around. Especially if he has something to hide."

I started the car. "I seriously doubt Dennis would have kept anything incriminating in his F & H office. My bet is, it's in his home office. Got time for a quick stop at Courtney's?"

"I wouldn't miss it," Pat said, settling back in her seat. "Let's just hope Glenn hasn't already gone by to search it."

* * *

"Why do you want to search Dennis's office?" Courtney asked.

We were standing in the living room, having just removed our coats. Courtney looked better than she had in a while. She had recently showered and dressed in clean clothes—an oversized Green Bay Packers sweatshirt and old, navy blue sweatpants. Despite the fact that both items were clearly too big for her, they still pulled against her swelling belly. Her face still showed the ravages of grief, but there was now a little peace mixed in, as well. Maybe her outburst during our call had helped her release some of her emotions. I hoped that was the case. In the background, I could hear Violet banging around in the kitchen, presumably making tea.

"I'd like to try and clear his name," I said. "That's what you want, right? Evidence he had nothing to do with Maple Leaf Grove or stealing from F & H? It's possible there's something in his office that can help us."

Her eyes widened. "You really think so?" Her voice was eager.

"It's certainly worth a try."

She nodded. "Of course, go ahead and look."

"Was anyone else in there?" I asked.

"The cops," she said, frowning. "They took some things, though I'm not sure what. I had to sign a paper."

My heart sank. Hopefully, they'd just focused on the brandy and packaging and left the files alone.

"I'll stay with you," Pat said, glancing at me.

"Oh." She seemed flustered. "You don't have to. My mom is here."

"That's okay," she said, tucking her arm through Courtney's. "I wanted to find out more about how you're doing. With the baby, and all. My mother died when I was pregnant with Barbara, and dealing with that grief was really rough." She patted Courtney's hand.

Courtney's face squished up. "Oh, I'm so sorry. I don't know what I'd do without my mother. And while you were pregnant … was Barbara your first?"

"She was," Pat said, leading Courtney to the couch and nodding at me over her head. I quickly disappeared down the hall

We had agreed in the car that Pat should stay in the living room with Courtney while I searched Dennis's office. Should we find something that implicated Dennis, we reasoned, neither of us wanted Courtney to wander in and find out. It seemed safer for me to search while Pat kept her busy.

Even though I had forgotten to ask Courtney where Dennis's office was, it was easy to find. As soon as I opened the door, I could tell. Oak wood paneling on the walls, hardwood floors covered with a thick bear rug, and a heavy, oak executive desk against the back wall pretty much screamed "man office." A black leather coach was pushed up against the opposite wall and a small cart for drinks stood nearby. Overstuffed bookcases lined the walls, although I didn't see any filing cabinets. I wondered if the cops took them, or if Dennis just didn't store many files at home. There didn't seem to be any room for filing cabinets anywhere else, so I thought it must be the latter.

I went around to his desk and started searching the drawers. The contents of the top drawer were typical: pens, paperclips, staples and whatnot. The next drawer slid out, displaying a tray of hanging files. I quickly searched through them, but they appeared to be personal. They were labeled "Insurance," "Warranties," "Receipts," and "Medical Bills." I didn't see anything labeled "Income" or "Tax," and wondered if the cops took those.

I closed that drawer and opened the next. This was another with hanging files, but they appeared to be stuffed with research. There were articles torn from magazines and newspapers, neatly labeled with the name of the periodical.

Frustrated, I slammed it shut. Now what?

I looked around the office. Even with the overstuffed bookcases, Dennis was surprisingly neat. Even the top of his desk was organized—there was one empty, stacked letter tray, a cup of pens, a phone, and one of those desk-pad calendars. It was December's, and it was filled with notes written in Dennis's careful hand. There were reminders of appointments outside the office along with what looked like general reminders.

Call Jim tomorrow.

Check out TG.

Ask Hans about records.

Hans. I kept staring at the name. Why was it so familiar?

"Knock, knock." Violet stuck her head inside the door, a smile on her face. "I thought you might like a nice cup of tea while you search."

I sat straight up. "Thank you. That would be lovely." I watched her as she came forward, holding the cup of tea carefully in front of her so she wouldn't spill.

"I wanted to thank you for everything you've been doing," she said. "I appreciate you looking after my daughter."

"Of course," I answered, taking the cup from her. "I'm happy to help."

She nodded her head slightly and turned to go, but I continued to talk, speaking in my normal voice. "Speaking of helping, why didn't you tell your daughter the truth about Tiffany and Dennis?"

She froze for a moment, before throwing a panicked glance over her shoulder. She hurried over to the office door and quietly asked, "Did you tell her?"

I didn't immediately answer. Instead, I simply watched her for a minute. Her face was frantic. "I did not," I finally said.

Relief swept her face. "Thank you," she breathed.

"Don't thank me," I said. "It was sheer luck I didn't mention it. Why didn't you tell me Courtney didn't know?"

Her cheeks flushed pink, and she ducked her head, seemingly unable to meet my gaze. "It was stupid not to tell you," she said. "Because you're right ... you easily could have mentioned something to Courtney. I guess ... I didn't want to get into why I didn't tell her."

"I don't understand," I said. "You wanted me to help, but you didn't want to tell me everything? You trust me to help, but not enough to give me an explanation? How do you expect me to be able to be of any use at all?"

She kept her eyes glued to the floor. "It was stupid," she said again, biting her lip. "I didn't want you to think badly of me. Of us."

I was floored. "Why would I think badly of either of you? Neither of you were doing the cheating."

Finally, Violet raised her head. "Because we were fools," she said, her voice bitter. "We should have known. I should have known. How did I miss the signs?"

"Why do you assume the affair was going on before Courtney was even in the picture?"

Her smile was rueful. "It's easier. Makes it worse to think it didn't start until he and Courtney were married, don't you think?"

I had to admit, she had a point.

"I felt so foolish," Violet continued. "I couldn't bear to tell you, or anyone else. I didn't think I could stand it if I felt like you were judging me. Even silently. I was already judging myself enough. How could I have let my daughter marry someone who was sleeping with his business partner's wife? And I was their secretary. How could I have not known what was going on?"

"Is that why you didn't tell Courtney?"

She bit her lip again and shook her head. "No. I didn't tell her because it would have broken her heart," she said, softly. "Even more than it already was. You have to understand. Courtney adored Tiffany. She would have done anything for her. Anything."

Anything but hide away when Dennis came to the club, like Tiffany told her to, I thought, but I held my tongue and let Violet continue.

"If she had known Tiffany was the one, I don't know what Courtney would have done. She was already in such a state when she found out. I was afraid it might push her over the edge."

Considering the fact that Courtney's reaction after finding out about Dennis's infidelity was to run out and jump in bed with another man, Violet had another point. At the same time, Nina's conviction that Dennis wasn't having an affair, much less with Tiffany, kept circling around in my head.

"How did you find out about the affair?" I asked.

She sighed. "I saw them."

"You saw Dennis and Tiffany?"

She nodded. "It was after my rotary club meeting. I was on the other side of town—normally, we do it at Fran's house, but she was in the middle of redoing her kitchen, so that day, we were at Gladys's—which was near Mario's ... have you been there? Cute little Italian restaurant. They have the best eggplant parmigiana. So, as I was driving by, I thought maybe I should treat myself to a late lunch—maybe even splurge on a glass of wine and skip dinner. I drove around the block, pulled into the parking lot, and got out of the car. I hadn't shut the door yet when I saw the restaurant door open and two people come out. It was Tiffany and Dennis. My first instinct was to start waving and calling out to them, to find out what they were doing at Mario's, but another instinct jumped in quick. I stayed where I was and watched them. As I did, I saw Tiffany lean closer and they ... they kissed."

Violet shuddered, shaking herself. "I couldn't stand watching it. I jumped back into my car, quietly shut the door, covered my face, and slid down in my seat, praying they wouldn't notice me. Tiffany didn't know what car I drove, but Dennis did. Luckily, I had parked near the back of the lot, next to an old pickup truck. I did that on purpose, you see, to force myself to walk a little further if I was going to have a big Italian lunch. Anyway, another car pulled into the parking lot. I could hear it, and I don't know if that distracted them or not, but shortly after, they got into their cars and left. As soon as I got myself under control, I left as well." She gave me a sideways smile. "I had lost my appetite."

I didn't respond. My mind was racing. Tiffany and Dennis were at a restaurant together in the middle of the day? That seemed to contradict what Nina believed, for sure. Although it seemed clear that Nina still loved Dennis, so I wondered if maybe part of what was going on was that she didn't want to believe that Tiffany and Dennis were sleeping together while they were married, too.

"Were you the one who told Courtney you saw Tiffany and Dennis?"

Violet hung her head again.

"I was beside myself," she said. "I didn't know what to do. I kept racking my brain, trying to remember if I had seen any indication of an affair when I was their secretary, but nothing came to mind. I knew I had to find a way to tell Courtney, but how? She had already been feeling restless, like something was off with her marriage. I kept telling her not to worry. Dennis was a busy man, after all. And it was natural after the first couple of years for things to mellow out. Building a life with someone is a lot different than the early days of a relationship when you're falling in love. She listened to me, but I could tell she was still bothered.

"The next day, she called me in tears. She had found lipstick on his shirt. So, of course, I had to tell her the truth, that I had seen him with a woman, but at the last moment, I couldn't tell her it was Tiffany. I lied and said I couldn't see the woman's face. She was silent for a moment, and then she just fell apart. She couldn't stop crying. I rushed over there and comforted her as best I could. She kept saying she felt like something was off with the marriage … that she had just known it."

"Did you encourage her to talk to Dennis? Or maybe get couples' therapy?"

"Not then. She was too upset. I told her she should get herself under control before she talked to Dennis. She promised she would. After a few days, she told me she had thought about it a lot and wanted to save her marriage, so she was going to focus on that. I told her I thought that was the right move, because she still loved him. And then Courtney got pregnant, and I thought maybe it was all going to work out. Dennis really seemed to be excited to be a father, and I hoped that meant he would also step up and take his marriage seriously. Then this happened."

It didn't sound to me like Violet had encouraged Courtney to deal with her relationship in a healthy, adult way. Inwardly, I sighed. No wonder Courtney had never spoken to Dennis about her suspicions.

"So, you don't think Dennis was seeing Tiffany anymore?"

Violet pressed her lips together in a flat line. "I don't know," she said. "Courtney didn't like talking about it. I hoped he wasn't, but I wasn't sure."

"You never saw anything else, though."

"No."

There was something about how stiffly she held herself, and how she continued to avert my eyes, that made me think she was holding something back. But what?

I decided to switch tactics. "So why did you tell me to talk to Tiffany?"

Her posture relaxed. This was something she was comfortable talking about. "Because I'm sure she's involved somehow. I just know it. But the police aren't looking at her."

"You think she poisoned Dennis? Her lover?"

"I didn't say that," Violet said. "I mean, it's possible. I'm not putting it past her. What I said was, 'I'm sure she's involved.'"

"Involved how?"

"Well, what if Glenn found out about the two of them?" she asked. "Glenn and Dennis have been friends for years. What a terrible betrayal it would be to find out his best friend and wife were sleeping together."

"So you think Glenn did it?"

"I think he's got more of a motive than my daughter," she said, her eyes full of steel and determination. "And I don't trust Tiffany at all. I think it's quite possible she threw Dennis under the bus to save her own marriage. Made him look worse. I could see Glenn wanting revenge."

Violet had a good point, although it made me wonder even more about Glenn. It sure seemed like no one liked him. Nina clearly didn't care for him, his own wife seemed to prefer Dennis, and now, Violet.

Although maybe that wasn't true. Maybe I was letting what Nina said earlier color my perception. Maybe I needed to talk to someone who had firsthand interactions with Glenn.

"When you worked for Glenn and Dennis, what was Glenn like?"

She looked a little surprised at the change of subject. "He was a good boss," she said. "He wasn't really friendly or anything. But he was fair. If you showed up and did your work efficiently, everything was fine."

"How was it between Dennis and Glenn?"

"Well, Dennis was definitely the charmer. He had the most clients and was the face of the company. Glenn was more behind the scenes. He was focused on the reports and whatnot. They seemed to make a good team—each had his own strengths and weaknesses, and they balanced each other out."

"Do you think it's possible Dennis would ever steal from the business?"

"Heaven's no." Violet shook her head furiously. "I can't see Dennis stealing from anyone. Although," her expression turned thoughtful. "I couldn't see him cheating on anyone, either. Regardless," she gave herself a little shake. "I don't see how he could. He had very little to do with the books and accounting. That was all Glenn."

That was the same thing Nina had said.

"What about Maple Leaf Grove? Do you think Dennis had anything to do with that?"

I was expecting the same answer as when I asked about Dennis stealing, but to my surprise, Violet hesitated. "Well, usually, Dennis was the one who brought the investment ideas to the table," she said slowly.

I sat up a little straighter.

"He was usually pretty good at finding the solid ones," she continued. "Not that all of them worked out, of course. He definitely had a few that didn't. But still, it would surprise me if he had anything to do with such a big miss. Not to mention that I can't imagine him hurting his clients like that."

"What about Glenn? Do you think the idea came from him?"

She frowned. "He was the numbers guy, although he would occasionally bring an idea to the office. Dennis would usually shoot it down, though." She half-smiled at the memory. "The rest of the staff would always stay away if that happened, because Glenn would invariably be grumpy. And a grumpy Glenn was not one anyone wanted to be around, especially if you had to report to him. I think he secretly wished he had Dennis's magic touch, when it came to investments."

I pushed the desk calendar closer to her. "What about these notes? Do any of them mean anything to you?"

She picked it up and turned it so she could read it. "There were a few Jims, at least while I was there. Not sure which one he was referring to. Hans ... that has to be Hans Christof."

Something in my head clicked. That was the name of the client who called Glenn the day I was there. "When I was meeting with Glenn, the secretary interrupted to let us know that Hans was on the phone. He was clearly upset."

"That's not entirely surprising." She handed the calendar back to me. "Hans was extremely detail-oriented, especially when it came to finances. He always knew how much he had in the bank, to the last penny. When F & H would send reports, he would go through them with a fine-toothed comb, and if he found any irregularities, he would call the office."

Was it possible that Hans was the one who discovered someone stealing from F & H?

She pursed her lips. "It is strange, though."

"What is?"

"Well, for Dennis to call him."

"Why, if Hans was a client?"

Violet shook her head. "That's the thing. He wasn't Dennis's client. He was Glenn's."

Chapter 16

Officer Brandon Wyle folded his arms across his broad chest and leaned back in his chair. "I thought you were here to tell me what you learned from Nina?"

"I am," I said impatiently. "This is part of it."

"What do allegations that Dennis stole from F & H have to do with Nina? Do you have some proof she was part of it?"

"Of course not. But Nina doesn't think Dennis was the one doing the stealing. And she isn't the only one."

Wyle lifted an eyebrow. "Who does she think is stealing, then?"

"Glenn."

"*Glenn*?" Wyle didn't look impressed. "If Glenn was stealing, why would he bring it up to us in the first place? Wouldn't he prefer not to draw attention to the stealing?"

"Not if someone found out." I pulled the folded calendar out of my purse and laid it on the table. "Look. See the note about Hans?"

"Where did you get this?"

"From Dennis's home office." I leaned over to point at the note. "Right there. That's Hans Christof, a long-term F & H client."

Wyle peered at it. "So?"

"So, Hans wasn't Dennis's client. He was Glenn's. And on the day that I was meeting with Glenn, his secretary came in to say that Hans was on the phone. She made it seem like he was upset."

Wyle glanced up at me. "None of that means anything. Hans could have been upset at any number of things. Including Dennis being murdered."

"Well, he wouldn't have been upset about Dennis being murdered when Dennis called him," I said. "Look, apparently Hans was very a detail-oriented client. He went over his reports very closely, and if he found any errors, he would call them out. What if he found some sort of irregularity, and when he brought it to F & H, Dennis began to realize something was wrong?"

Wyle dug under one of his towering piles of paper and pulled out a notebook and pen. "So, you think Glenn killed Dennis because he was going to find out Glenn was stealing from the company?"

"It makes sense, if you think about it," I said. "Glenn actually had a lot of reasons to want to kill Dennis. Between the affair with Tiffany and trying to cover up the stealing, he appears to be a more likely suspect than Courtney."

Wyle was busy writing notes. "IF Glenn was stealing. There's no evidence of that."

"That's why I was thinking you could call Hans and ask him."

Wyle glanced up at me. "You didn't talk to him?"

"Well, I tried," I said. "He didn't answer his phone. But I think it might be better coming from you anyway. If he is one of those who dots the I's and crosses the T's, he would probably feel more comfortable talking to someone official."

"I'll give him a call," Wyle said. "So, Nina thought Glenn was stealing?"

"Nina thought it was far more likely Glenn was stealing than Dennis," I said. "She also thought that the whole Maple Leaf Grove fiasco was more likely Glenn's fault than Dennis's, which, again, with Dennis gone, he does make a much better scapegoat. In all fairness, though, I feel like I should add that it's possible she's biased."

"Why? Because they were married? I would think that would make her more biased *against* Dennis."

"True, but in this case, I think she's still in love with him."

Wyle made another note in his notebook. "Anything else?"

I shifted uncomfortably in my seat. "Well ..."

Wyle gave me another look. "Charlie?"

"It's just ... Nina didn't think it likely that Dennis was having an affair with Tiffany."

Wyle stared at me for a moment, then put down his pen. "She didn't think it was likely that Dennis was having an affair at all, or that it was with Tiffany?"

"Both, actually. She thinks he's married to his work and can barely handle one relationship, much less something on the side. And, if he was going to cheat, Tiffany wouldn't be the one he'd choose."

Wyle pondered this. "What do you think?"

I sighed. "Quite honestly, I don't really know. Violet, Courtney's mother, is the one who saw them together. They were at Mario's in the middle of the day. Why would they be together like that if there wasn't something going on between them? Yet Nina was adamant. They all knew each other in college, and according to Nina, Tiffany had the hots for Dennis from the moment she laid eyes on him, but he didn't have the same feelings for her."

"Then why did she marry Glenn?"

"Nina didn't know for sure, but she guessed it was to stay close to Dennis. Nina made Tiffany out to be a bit of an obsessive stalker."

Wyle grew very still. "Obsessive enough to have killed Dennis?"

"Wouldn't she have more likely killed Courtney, in that case?"

"You'd be surprised," Wyle said drily. "It's not like obsessive people are particularly stable, and sometimes they decide if they can't have the object of their obsession, no one can."

I thought about it. "With Courtney being so pregnant, that does change things. Courtney would always be part of his life, even if they eventually divorced. Unlike Nina. So, Tiffany would have been less threatened by Nina than Courtney."

"It's also possible Dennis ended it," Wyle said. "The baby will arrive soon. Maybe he told Tiffany that it was over. And she, realizing that she was never going to get Dennis, became so furious that she killed him."

"She also does know her herbs," I said. "And she has re-lationships with businesses that sell herbs, so she could have purchased Monkshood."

Wyle gave me a look. "I guess I shouldn't be surprised you also know Monkshood can be purchased."

"I should say not," I said archly. "Making teas IS what I do."

"So you keep telling me," Wyle said. He jotted down anoth-er few notes. "Anything else?"

"Other than I hope you're no longer laser-focused on Court-ney?" I asked. "I think it's pretty clear by now that there are other suspects."

"If I tell you we're following up on other leads, will you stay out of it?"

"Probably," I said.

Wyle rolled his eyes.

"Okay then," I said, gathering my coat and preparing to leave. "I will leave you to your investigations."

Wyle sat back. "You do know that what you found out could still implicate Courtney, don't you?"

I paused and gave him a hard look. "In what way?"

Wyle tapped his pen on his desk. "Well, you still have Dennis cheating on Courtney. What if Dennis didn't end things with Tiffany, but he did with Courtney?"

I stilled. "What makes you think that happened?"

"Oh come on, Charlie," Wyle said. "You're not going to tell me you didn't know about Luke Zellner."

I closed my eyes.

Wyle nodded. "That's what I thought."

"How did you find out?" I asked.

"I should be asking YOU that."

"He came to see me," I said. "He's the one who told me about Maple Leaf Grove and that maybe one of Dennis's clients took revenge."

Wyle made some notes. "Did you know one of Luke's many jobs is gardening and yard work? Apparently, he's pretty good about it. One of his clients," at this, Wyle made a show of flip-ping back through his pages. "Ah, yes. A Mrs. Little. She loves her flowers. Has a huge flower garden that Luke helps her with every summer. Want to guess what's in that garden?"

I sat back down in my chair. "Monkshood."

Wyle nodded.

"How did you even figure this out?" I asked. "It's not like Monkshood is growing right now."

He flashed a grin at me. "Superior detective work."

I rolled my eyes.

"Actually, you helped with that," he conceded. "Your comment about how people grew it because it has beautiful flowers stuck with me, and I made a few calls to local nurseries. I got a list of avid flower-growers, including Mrs. Little, and went around to ask them about their gardens. Imagine my surprise when I discovered that Luke was her helper."

"As you pointed out, that's hardly proof of Luke putting the Monkshood in Dennis's brandy," I said. "Lots of people have Monkshood in their gardens."

"That's true, but not all of them know how poisonous it is. Mrs. Little did. She knows her flowers. And she made sure to tell Luke."

"That's still not proof," I said. "And, even so, it seems to implicate Luke more than Courtney."

"They could have done it together," he said.

"None of this gets Glenn off the hook," I countered. "If he's stealing from the company, or he's the one to blame for Maple Leaf, that gave him a powerful motive to get rid of Dennis."

"Or, Courtney could be trying to avoid financial issues," he said. "If F & H is going down because of Glenn's actions, Dennis would have been taken down with it. But with Dennis gone, if it can be proven it was all Glenn, then she'll likely be financially set. That could be another reason why Luke is trying to point the finger at Glenn."

I wasn't at all happy with the direction Wyle was going. "I don't know," I said. "Luke didn't strike me as a killer."

Wyle raised an eyebrow. "Oh? Are you familiar with many killers?"

"That's beside the point," I countered.

"I disagree," Wyle said. "I think that *is* the point."

"Actually, the point is, are you going to look at anyone other than Courtney?"

"Everyone is a suspect," he said.

"That's not an answer."

"We haven't eliminated anyone, if that's what you're asking," he said. "We're keeping our options open."

Clearly, that was all I was going to get out of Wyle. I stood up again to leave. "Oh, real quick … how did you find out about Luke?"

Wyle flashed that grin again. "Actually, I wasn't sure. We knew Courtney and Luke were friends, but we didn't know there was anything else going on. So, thank you for confirming that."

Mentally, I kicked myself. First the gardening, and now the affair. Some private detective I was turning out to be.

As dignified as I could manage it, I turned on my heel and left the room.

"Thanks again, Charlie," Wyle called out, a hint of laughter in his voice. I ignored him.

* * *

I pulled open the door of Fit for Life. I knew I was taking a chance, but I felt like I had no choice.

While I had hoped Wyle would investigate Glenn and his financial dealings, I couldn't be sure. I also couldn't be sure he wouldn't try and turn the whole thing around on Courtney.

I needed something else. Some other proof that would point to someone else.

And all my instincts were screaming that Tiffany held the key.

I knew she was hiding something. That was clear. The question was, what?

Jillian was standing by the front desk again. "Hello and welcome!" she said, her voice cheery. "Are you a member?"

"Actually, I'm here to see Tiffany," I said. "I'm the one selling teas. I met with her a couple of weeks ago about it." Inwardly, I held my breath. Based on what I had seen of their relationship, I didn't think Tiffany would have confided to Jillian that I was really poking around for Courtney's sake, but I couldn't be sure.

Jillian studied me for a second before her face cleared. "Of course. I remember you now." Her face puckered in a frown. "I don't know if she's available or not."

"That's okay," I said, as I strode forward. "It won't take long. I'll just see if I can find her myself."

I walked over to Tiffany's office. The door was open a crack, but not quite enough for me to see if she was inside. I gently pushed it open a tiny bit further.

There she was, sitting at her desk, staring off into space. "I thought I told you to always knock, Jillian," she said, without looking.

I pushed it open a little further while simultaneously knocking.

She rolled her eyes and looked over at me. They widened as soon as she recognized me. "You have some nerve showing your face here," she said firmly.

I held my hands out. "Do you have a few minutes? I know I have no right to ask, but it's important."

Tiffany pressed her lips together so tightly, they turned white. She really didn't look well. Her face was plastered with makeup, even more thickly than the last time I saw her, but it still didn't hide how pale and greenish she looked, or the dark circles under her eyes.

"Glenn told me you were trouble," she said. "You were using me to get to him."

"Please, Tiffany," I said. "It will only take a moment. And if you don't want to see me again, you won't have to."

She looked away, visibly fighting with herself. I held my breath again. If she threw me out without speaking to me, I wasn't sure what I was going to do. I just had to hope I had read the situation between her and Glenn correctly.

"Fine," she spat. "You have five minutes. No more."

"Thank you," I said, easing my way into her office. I closed the door behind me and weaved my way through the piles of paper before seating myself in the chair in front of her.

She stared at me, her green eyes no longer intense, but dull and listless instead. "Well, what is it?"

"What do you know about the financial situation at F & H?"

Her expression turned wary. "What do you mean?"

"Has Glenn talked to you about what's going on?"

She dropped her gaze to her desk. "You mean that Dennis was stealing from the business?"

"Yes. Except … what if it wasn't Dennis?"

Her face snapped up. "What are you talking about?"

"What if it was Glenn?"

A mixture of emotions played out on her face. "Glenn?"

I nodded, watching her carefully.

"That doesn't make any sense," she said. "Glenn would never do that."

"And Dennis would?"

"Dennis was desperate."

"Desperate? How so?"

She looked away. "Because of Maple Leaf."

I leaned forward slightly. "Did Glenn tell you that Dennis was desperate?"

"He didn't want to," Tiffany said, biting her lip. "He said that he felt terrible about what Dennis was going through. But unfortunately, Dennis's choices really hurt us. He said he didn't blame Dennis, because he was sure Dennis wasn't intending to cause us harm. He was just trying to take care of his family, but as the saying goes … 'The road to hell is paved with good intentions.'"

"Dennis didn't actually lose any money with Maple Leaf."

Tiffany looked confused. "Of course he did. Everyone did."

I shook my head. "No. That's why some of their clients thought Dennis knew it was a bad investment … because he purposefully didn't put much money into it."

Tiffany was shaking her head. "But that can't be. You must be mistaken. I mean, yes, someone at F & H messed up on the due diligence, it's true. But both Dennis and Glenn were fooled, and they both lost money. Dennis, unfortunately, made another bad choice to steal from the business, but that has nothing to do with the clients. That just affects us. I know the clients are upset, but it was because it was a bad investment, and as it was Dennis's idea, of course they blame him."

"No, that's really not true," I said quietly. "I can give you a list of clients who are furious at Dennis because he *didn't* invest very much of his own money. It has nothing to do with whose idea it was."

The color was starting to drain from Tiffany's face. "That can't be," she whispered.

The more I watched her, the sorrier I felt for her, and the more terrible I felt about what I was doing. It was like I was torturing her. But if she didn't tell me what she knew, Courtney would be the one who would suffer. And I couldn't have that.

"Here's what I think happened," I said. "I think Glenn was always a little jealous of Dennis. Dennis was the star of the business. He was the one who was great at sales, but even more than that, he also had a knack for finding the hot investments. I think Glenn wanted a little of that star power for himself. So, he went out and found Maple Leaf Grove. Dennis wasn't so sure about it, but Glenn was able to persuade him to go along with it. I'm not sure how—hopefully, he didn't go as far as to doctor any analyses, but who knows? Dennis was never completely convinced, which is why he didn't invest much of his own money, but also didn't stand in the way of Glenn presenting it to his clients. It's possible Dennis even told a few of his clients about it.

"When the whole thing crashed, that's when Glenn became desperate. He was probably invested heavily in the project, right?"

Tiffany was staring at the DON'T QUIT poster. "Nearly all we had," she said quietly. "He said he knew it would be tight for us for a few years, but it would be worth it. Once it paid off, we wouldn't have to worry about money anymore."

She looked so forlorn, I wanted to reach out and squeeze her hand. Instead, I took a deep breath and continued. "So, that's when he probably decided to steal from the business," I said. "And he probably did it for the same reasons he told you Dennis did it. For his family. For you. But unfortunately for him, he was found out. My guess is, he was taking money from the client accounts—not much, just a little bit from all of them—but some of the clients discovered it and told Dennis about it. Glenn had to do something, and my guess is he thought the best way to make it all go away was to get rid of Dennis. Then he could blame Dennis for the theft as well as the Maple Leaf mess, and start to rebuild the business and his finances from there."

Tiffany shook her head. "You're wrong," she said. "Glenn would never do any of that. It had to be Dennis."

"Tiffany, think," I said. "Dennis didn't have access to the accounting and the books the way Glenn did. Do you really think Dennis could have stolen from the business without Glenn knowing about it?"

She kept shaking her head. "I don't believe it," she said. "I've known Glenn for years. You've barely met him. He's a good man. He would never do anything like that."

"But Tiffany ..."

"You need to go now," she said flatly. "Your five minutes is up."

I wanted to protest, but her face had completely shut down. It was clear she was done listening.

I stood to leave. "Think long and hard about what you're doing, Tiffany," I said quietly. "There is a pregnant woman who is in real danger of going to jail over something she didn't do. Not only will her life be ruined, but so will her unborn child's. Will you be able to look at yourself in the mirror if you allow it?"

"If you don't leave now, I'm going to call the cops," she said, picking up her phone. "You have five seconds to get out of my office."

I picked my way toward the door, accepting defeat. My only hope was that my words had hit a weak spot, and that they'd keep poking at her until she did something about it.

Chapter 17

I was sound asleep when the loud jangle of the phone jarred me awake.

Disoriented, I flung an arm out, whacking Midnight, who was peacefully sleeping on the pillow. He let out an annoyed hiss, which made me think there was someone in the room with me … until I realized it was the phone ringing.

I rolled over and stared bleary-eyed at the clock radio. It was nearly one in the morning. Terrified it was my sister Annabelle with some sort of devastating family news, I snatched up the phone.

"Hello?"

Silence.

"Hello?" I said again as I started to question myself. Had the phone even been ringing, or was it something else? No—there was no dial tone, so someone was obviously on the other line. "Hello?"

Was this some sort of prank? I was starting to get annoyed and was taking a deep breath to give whoever was on the other end of the line an earful when I heard it—the muffled sound of crying.

"Who is this?" I asked, keeping my voice as gentle as possible. "Courtney, is that you?" Oh no … had she been arrested? Was there a problem with the baby? Thoughts swirled through my head.

I was about to tell Courtney to hang on, I would be there in a jiffy, when a shaky voice answered. "Not … Courtney."

I couldn't recognize it, as it was too thick with tears. Pat, maybe? I didn't think so, but I couldn't tell. "I'm here," I said. "Let me know what you need."

"I … I did it."

I sat straight up in bed, the last vestiges of sleep disappearing from my mind. "What did you do?"

"Glenn. I did it."

Suddenly, the pieces clicked together. "Tiffany?"

"After I found it, I called the cops."

"Wait, found what? Tiffany, what's going on? Where's Glenn?"

"Not ... not here."

"Then where?"

"At the station."

My eyes widened. Fully awake, I threw the covers off the bed. "I'll be right over."

* * *

It took me longer than I wanted, mostly because I had to look up Tiffany's address in the phonebook and then find it on a map. Tiffany was clearly not in any state to give me directions. I threw on the same pair of jeans and sweater I had worn earlier, grabbed the map, my keys, and a bag of lavender chamomile tea, and headed out.

Tiffany and Glenn lived in a large house in a quiet cul-de-sac. Even in the dark, I could tell it was larger and fancier than Dennis's home. I couldn't help but wonder again what Glenn really thought of Dennis. Were they really friends, as Dennis seemed to believe? Or had Glenn spent years quietly seething, feeling like a second-class citizen? After all, everyone loved Dennis, including, it seemed, his own wife. I almost felt sorry for him, having to hide his true feelings from everyone. Yet no matter how deep he buried them, they would reveal themselves in tiny ways ... as in the size of his house.

Then again, thinking about the damage he had apparently done to so many lives, I didn't feel quite so sorry.

Tiffany opened the door as I approached the porch. She was dressed in a bright-yellow tracksuit that was stained across the front, and her face was red and blotchy from tears. She was not a pretty crier.

She didn't say anything, just left the door open and walked away, weaving slightly. I wondered if she had been drinking.

I followed her into the house, closing the door behind me and hanging up my coat. The lights were off, and she barely responded when I called out, so it took a bit of stumbling around before I finally found her in the kitchen.

She was sitting at the table, a half-empty bottle of vodka in front of her alongside a glass. "Want some?" she asked, lifting the bottle toward me.

I shook my head, even though she wasn't looking at me. "I brought some tea," I said. "Would it be okay if I made a pot?"

"Suit yourself," she answered, taking a swig straight from the bottle.

"Can I turn on a light?" Even though my eyes were adjusting to the dimness, having the light on in an unfamiliar home would make things easier. It also might help me get Tiffany sobered up.

Tiffany shrugged, which I took as a "yes." I found the lightswitch and flipped it on. Tiffany shied away from the glare, putting both her hands up to cover her face while making a little "oof" noise. I didn't respond, instead heading further into the kitchen.

I couldn't find a teapot, so I prepared two mugs and brought them over to the table, placing one in front of Tiffany. Dully, she stared at me, but didn't move.

"So, what happened?" I asked, sitting down across from her.

Tiffany's throat contracted as she swallowed a couple of times, preparing to speak. "I kept thinking about what you said," she explained quietly, her voice still thick with tears and vodka. "Glenn, he ... I had my suspicions something was wrong. For a while now. Months. I felt like he hadn't been telling me the whole truth. I brushed it off, though. When the news broke on Maple Leaf ..." she shook her head. "It was awful. I thought Glenn was going to have a heart attack. He was completely out of control, drinking and pacing. Frankly, it terrified me. Glenn doesn't lose control. He just doesn't, but that night ..." She paused and chewed on her lip.

"Well, after that night, he was still really stressed, but he seemed better. More like Glenn. So, I wrote off those uneasy feelings I'd had as Glenn just being stressed and trying to fix things. He assured me he had a plan. He was going to find a way to replace our savings. We might have to tighten our belts for a little while, but he was going to take care of it. And I believed him. I'm such an idiot." At that, she reached for the bottle to take another drink.

"You love him," I said. "Of course you want to believe the best about him. There's nothing wrong, shameful, or stupid about that."

She let out a bark of laughter. "That's what makes everything even worse. I *don't* love him. I never have." She bowed her head, but not before I saw the sheen of tears in her eyes again.

"Why did you marry him if you didn't love him?"

"Because, again, I'm an idiot," she said. She blew the air out of her cheeks and raised her head to meet my eyes. "You probably already knew that, anyway. I don't know why I bother to hide it. Why I bother to hide anything. I'm such a fool." Her voice was bitter.

"We all make mistakes," I said. "You're human."

She muttered something. "I guess it doesn't matter anymore. Nothing matters. It's not like I'll ever be with him now, anyway."

"You're talking about Dennis."

Her lips curled into a cynical, self-loathing smile. "See? I knew you knew."

I reached for my tea and took a sip, hoping it would encourage Tiffany to do the same. "So, what happened?"

She didn't say anything for a moment, just kept staring at something off in the distance. "I fell in love with Dennis the moment I laid eyes on him." She said, her voice warm with the memory. "We were all in college. I was dating Glenn at the time, and it was fine. I wasn't in love with him or anything like that, but he was nice to me. Treated me well. Which I really liked, because before him, my boyfriend had been awful to me. Just terrible. So Glenn was a nice change. But when I met Dennis, everything shifted. I knew, in my heart, that he was my soulmate. But at the time, we were both with someone else.

"So, I waited, figuring he would eventually break up with Nina, and then I would break up with Glenn, and we would be together. He and Nina had such a volatile relationship; I assumed it was just a matter of time. As much as I could, I focused on being a good friend to Dennis, figuring that the more time I spent with him, the more likely it was that he would wake up and realize we were meant to be. But of course, that didn't happen. He got engaged to Nina.

"I was so depressed when that happened. I didn't know what to do. All I could think about was how much I had wasted my life. And for what? The love of my life was going to marry someone else.

"I spent the weekend hiding in my apartment, refusing to go out, binging on wine, ice cream, and bad television. By Monday, I had pulled myself together enough to go back to work, but I still couldn't stand to see anyone. For the next couple of weeks, all I did was go to work, come home, and spend my evenings eating way too much sugar and drinking way too much alcohol.

"In the middle of all of this, Glenn stopped by one night and asked me to marry him. I was completely and utterly shocked. He said he could tell I wasn't myself, and he thought it was because Dennis had asked Nina to marry him ... he thought I was upset that he hadn't asked me yet! I was so flabbergasted, I ended up saying 'yes.' He was excited and wanted to stay and celebrate, but I managed to utter something about being sick and having a big day. I asked if we could celebrate that weekend. He agreed and left.

"I spent two days in a fog, wondering what I had just agreed to. I decided to tell Glenn I was sorry, but I couldn't marry him after all. Then, after I did that, I would pack up and move as far away as I could possibly get from this town. Maybe a fresh start was what I needed—somewhere with no Glenn or Dennis. Maybe I'd even eventually find someone new.

"But then Saturday night came, and Glenn showed up at my apartment. He was so happy, all dressed up and everything. He even had a ring with him. It felt like the words were stuck in my throat. He slid the ring onto my finger and whisked me off to a fancy restaurant. I remember sitting there at the table, watching Glenn eat his steak as I picked at my salmon, telling myself I had to do it. I had to tell him the truth. The longer I kept up the charade, the harder it was going to be on him. I wasn't even listening to him talk. I was so busy trying to steel myself to tell him the truth, and then I heard the words 'Dennis' and 'broken engagement.'

"Of course, that got my attention, and I asked him to repeat himself. What had happened was that Dennis and Nina had gotten into a huge fight and nearly broke off their engagement. Then, I remember Glenn shaking his head as he said, 'I don't know why Dennis puts up with it. All they do is fight. Doesn't he know he's setting himself up for a big divorce settlement?'

"And it was like lightning struck me. It wasn't over yet. Dennis still had Nina in his system, but once he was finally finished with her, I would be there for him, just as I had planned. Yes, it would be a little messier to divorce Glenn versus just breaking up with him, but so what? It would be worth it, if I could have Dennis in the long run. So I decided, at least in the short term, to keep the engagement going."

Tiffany paused to take another drink, her expression haunted and brooding.

"So, what happened when Dennis divorced Nina?" I asked. "Why didn't you leave Glenn then?"

She didn't answer for a moment, as she swallowed more vodka. Then, replacing the bottle to the table with a thud, she said, "He didn't want me."

My eyes widened, and I tried to hide my surprise. "You didn't have an affair with him?"

"We slept together a few times, if that's what you mean. While he was separated from Nina. But it was clear, even then, that he wasn't interested in a long-term relationship with me.

He kept saying he felt guilty cheating on his friend and business partner, but I knew the truth."

"But what about Courtney?"

She laughed, but it was an empty laugh, dark and void of humor. "Courtney. I had a bad feeling about her from the start. She was so different from Nina, just completely opposite, and I just knew ..." She shook her head. "I knew he wanted a family. He wanted kids and a wife who would stay home and take care of the family. I kept telling him if that's what he wanted, I could do it. I always wanted kids. Glenn never really did. I would have happily stayed home if it meant I could have Dennis and a family. But for some reason, Dennis didn't believe me. Or maybe he just didn't want to believe me. Every time it came up, he would just laugh and tell me I would last a year, maybe two, and then I would want to go back to work. He said there was nothing wrong with that, but he wanted something else. Anyway, Courtney just oozes stay-at-home mom energy. So, I tried to keep them from meeting. At the time, I was still trying to convince Dennis that I was the one for him. But Courtney didn't listen to me. The one time she decided not to listen. I was so angry with her, I nearly fired her on the spot. But I knew that wouldn't help me win back Dennis. So I kept my mouth shut. It didn't matter, though. None of it mattered. He fell in love with her, and that was it."

"So, the affair didn't continue after he married Courtney?"

Tiffany shook her head.

"But ... someone saw you two."

She jerked her head over to stare at me. "What are you talking about?"

She seemed genuinely bewildered. I was starting to wonder if Violet had been seeing things that day, although Courtney had also talked about Dennis having lipstick on his collar.

"You were at Mario's with him? And when you left, you kissed?"

Her expression was incredulous. "Someone saw *that*?"

I nodded.

"I guess they didn't see him pull away from me, and tell me it was over. He didn't have feelings for me like that. He said I should focus on my own marriage."

My eyes widened. "Ah, no. They definitely didn't see that."

"Figured."

"But why were you even at Mario's to begin with, if there wasn't anything going on?"

"A mistake," she spat. "A stupid mistake. I was meeting a friend there for lunch, but she never showed up. She got the day wrong, and Dennis had a business meeting cancel. The hostess had seated us near each other, and when we realized we were both going to sit alone, we decided to eat together. Dennis had ordered a bottle of wine, and silly me … I had some."

She squeezed her eyes shut, like the memory was painful. "We had such a nice, relaxing lunch. He was funny and charming. I was sure it was a sign from the universe that we were going to be together. He had come to his senses and finally realized he was supposed to be with me."

She pressed her lips together. "I've done so many stupid things in my life, but this one takes the cake. After leaving the restaurant, I hugged and kissed him, sure we were about to rekindle our affair. After he got over the initial shock, though, he pushed me away. Told me it was over. It was never going to happen."

"I'm sorry," I said, even though I wasn't sure if it was the appropriate thing to say in the situation or not. Was I really sorry that she wasn't able to convince a man to cheat on his wife? No. But her grief and sadness were so real and so powerful, I felt like I had to say something. And I *was* sorry she had suffered so.

She shrugged. "Doesn't matter now. He's gone. Glenn is gone. It's all gone."

Her voice was hollow and empty, sending a chill up my spine. "You said Glenn was at the station. You mean the police station?"

She nodded. "I couldn't stop thinking about the last year. How stressed Glenn had been. How everything kept unraveling, even though he kept saying he had it all under control. And I kept thinking about what you said. Was it possible that Glenn, not Dennis, was the one to blame for all the financial issues?"

She paused and swallowed hard. "I couldn't stand it, so on Wednesday, I told Jillian I had to run an errand and to keep an eye on things. I went home. Glenn was at work, so it was a good time to go through his desk. It was ..." she closed her eyes. "It was worse than I thought. Credit cards are maxed. Bills are overdue. The more I dug, the sicker I got. But then, at the bottom of all the mess, I found some bank statements of Glenn's cousin, who died a couple of years ago. I didn't think anything of it at first—Glenn was the executor of his will, but as I was about to set them aside, something caused me to look a little closer. I saw that the account was opened a few months ago, in October. How did that happen, when his cousin is dead? And the account was set up at a bank in Riverview, but the address was a PO box in Redemption. His cousin lived in Milwaukee ... not that it even matters, considering he is dead. Dead people don't typically open up new bank accounts. I looked at the balance, and it was over *twenty thousand dollars*. I couldn't believe it. Did Glenn open an account with his cousin's name at a bank in a different town and put all this money in it? Why would he do that? Why wasn't he using the money to pay our bills?

"When he got home that night, we had a huge fight about it. He was furious that I had 'violated his trust' by digging around in his desk. He kept saying I needed to trust him, even though I had found a secret bank account! I started to think he was going to leave me and was hiding money, but he kept assuring me over and over that no, he loved me, and he was hiding the money for my own good. He kept repeating how I needed to trust him.

"Anyway, I couldn't stop thinking about that bank account and how he was depositing money regularly into it but not paying our bills. And then, I got to thinking, what if he WAS stealing money from the business, but he was trying to cover his tracks? No one would be looking for an account under his cousin's name. Was that what he was doing?

"Then, I started to think about Dennis's death, and the fact that it was supposedly Dennis's cousin who sent him the poisoned bottle. And how the poison was actually an herb. So, I called my herbalists to see if any of them had any orders for Monkshood sent to Redemption."

My uneasy feeling increased. "And did they?"

She nodded, her eyes filling up with tears. "Yes."

I sucked in my breath. "Did they tell you who ordered it?"

She turned her head to look at me. "Me."

"You?" My mouth dropped open in astonishment. "How is that possible?"

"I have an account, and it was charged to that."

"But ... how?"

She shook her head. "I don't know. I talked to the owner, but the order was placed over a month ago. As far as anyone is concerned, I am the one who ordered it."

I frowned. "But that couldn't have been Glenn, then. Glenn doesn't sound anything like you."

"I don't know if they wrote down the name of who ordered it, or if it's all just under my account," Tiffany said. "Jillian orders things for me all the time, but when I get a bill, there's nothing on it as to who ordered what ... just a list of dates and items in the shipment."

"But how would Glenn have gotten that information without you knowing?" I asked. "And wouldn't the order have come to Fit for Life? You would have seen the box."

She sighed. "Again, the record-keeping isn't great. I asked them where they shipped it, but they don't have any kind of real paper trail. It's entirely possible that whoever called it in simply requested it be sent to a PO box. It wasn't just Monkshood in the order, either. There were other things, too. Essential oils, homemade soaps, and candles. My guess is whoever put the order in told them it was supposed to be a surprise."

"Some surprise ... one you even paid for," I mused.

Her smile was twisted. "Well, we are married, so would it really matter anyhow? Quite honestly, I would never have known if I hadn't called. Glenn does my books. I don't even look at the bills they send. I just bring them home, hand them to Glenn, and he pays for them. I never would have been the wiser, otherwise."

The longer I listened, the more I had to hand it to Glenn. He had thought of nearly everything. If he had just handled stealing from the business a little better, he probably would have gotten away with it all, and Courtney would be sitting in the police station rather than him.

"I take it you told the cops all this," I said.

She nodded. "Glenn kept telling me it was all a mistake. He didn't do it. He didn't even know what Monkshood was." Her gaze slid off me, staring at nothing, her face numb with grief and pain. "But after all the lies, how can I possibly believe him anymore?"

"You did the right thing," I said.

Her lips curled in disgust. "Not really," she said. "When it comes right down to it, I was more than willing to let Courtney go to jail to save my marriage. Well, not my marriage per se, but my lifestyle. Deep down, I knew there was something dreadfully wrong. There were all these little things I kept ignoring, but once I had the proof in front of me, I realized I couldn't turn a blind eye anymore. It's not just how stressed he was last fall. He wasn't even that upset when we got the news that Dennis was murdered. He just went back to work like nothing had happened. And there was the day I found one of my herb reference books on my nightstand, even though I was sure I hadn't put it there. I even asked Glenn about it, but he said it was me, of course. I read a lot of magazines and books, and every time I see a new herb, I look it up, but I don't remember doing that. I just brushed it off, sure he was right … figured I had just forgotten I'd moved it. I do that a lot, as well … move things around and forget where I put them. But deep down, I knew there was something else going on. And now, I have to live with the fact that I was willing to let an innocent person go to jail—an innocent pregnant woman—because I didn't want to be inconvenienced."

I had no answer. There was nothing I could think of that didn't sound like worthless, empty platitudes. Instead, I did the one thing I had wanted do since I walked into her house. I pulled my chair closer to Tiffany's and put my arms around her. She was stiff as a board at first, but after a few minutes, she melted into me, laying her head against my chest and bawling like a baby.

Chapter 18

"So it was Glenn after all," Pat said.

"It seems so," I replied, tucking the phone between my neck and ear as I got the kettle boiling. I was exhausted. After Tiffany had her cry, which took a while, she let me lead her to the bedroom, docile and wrung out, and tuck her into bed. She was asleep before I even left the room.

Unfortunately for me, sleep eluded me. Locking Tiffany's door behind me, I drove home and climbed back into my own bed, alongside Midnight who was still curled up on a pillow. But all I could do was stare at the ceiling, puzzling over what Tiffany had told me.

Something wasn't right. I just couldn't put my finger on it.

"Well, he certainly is the most obvious suspect," Pat said. "Wasn't it Agatha Christie who said the obvious suspect is usually the one who did it?"

"Like anything Agatha Christie wrote was obvious," I muttered. "But yes, it does appear like Glenn had the most to gain. It makes the most sense."

"I guess we were wrong about poison being a woman's weapon," Pat mused. "That's really the only thing that doesn't completely fit."

I dragged a kitchen chair closer to the phone, so I didn't have to stretch out the cord so much, and sat down heavily, tea in hand. "I know. It's still sort of gnawing at me."

"But it's not like it could be anyone else," Pat continued. "I mean, who else would have known about Tiffany's herb distributor, and that she had an account there? It has to be Glenn."

"Yeah, it does seem likely," I said, wishing my head wasn't so foggy from lack of sleep. Something still wasn't adding up. All these details that only a handful of people would know. Dennis's favorite brandy. His relationship to his cousin. An out-of-town herb distributor who sold Monkshood.

Who would have known all those things?

"You don't sound convinced," Pat said.

"It's probably just because I'm exhausted," I said. "I probably just need to catch up on my sleep."

"I'm sure that's it," Pat said, although her tone sounded like she believed it about as much as I did.

* * *

"Charlie," Violet said, a huge smile on her face as she opened the door to her apartment. "Come in! It's so nice to see you."

"Thank you," I said, stepping inside and removing my coat. "Do you have a few moments?"

"Of course, of course," she said, bustling toward the kitchen. "I always have time for the woman who saved my daughter from jail. I'll go make some tea."

I hung my coat up and followed her into the kitchen. Her apartment was small but neat as a pin. The kitchen was cheery with accents of reds, yellows, oranges, and lots of roosters.

"Come sit," she said, holding a couple of bright-orange mugs with yellow flowers and placing them on the kitchen table. I sat as she brought out a tin of shortbread cookies. "I just love these," she said. "Have a few, so I don't eat all of them."

Obediently, I chose one, although I didn't take a bite. She didn't notice as she put a couple on her plate. "So, what can I do for you?" she asked. Then, her eyes went wide. "Oh! Did you want some money? I know you said you didn't when you first started helping us, but if you've changed your mind ..."

I waved my hand. "No, I'm fine. That's not why I'm here. I actually had a few more questions."

"Fire away," she said.

I paused, giving myself a moment to organize my thoughts. "Did you ever ask Dennis about what you saw?"

Violet looked at me in confusion, her smile faltering. "Saw?"

"Yes. The day you saw him and Tiffany at Mario's."

"What does that matter now?"

I smiled at her reassuringly. "Indulge me."

Her expression became wary. "Well, no. What would be the point? He would just lie." Her tone was bitter.

I nodded. "Yes, that does seem likely. Although, when I asked Tiffany about it two nights ago, she denied their having an affair while he was married to Courtney."

Her mouth flattened. "Well, of course she would."

"Really?" Now it was my turn to look confused. "Why would she lie now?"

"Well, she's married," Violet said, as if it were obvious. "She doesn't want her husband to find out."

"Her husband is charged with killing her lover," I said. "Do you think it matters now if he knows about the affair?"

She flapped her hands. "Well, it still makes her look bad, right? I mean, who wants to admit she had an affair?"

I picked up the mug to take a sip and tried not to make a face. Ugh. Store-bought. "That's true. I'm sure it would be difficult to admit to having an affair."

She sat back, her expression relaxing.

"Except," I continued pleasantly, watching the muscles in her face tense up again. "She DID admit to having an affair with Dennis."

"I thought you just said she didn't?"

"While he was married to Courtney, Tiffany wasn't," I said. "Nor while he was married to Nina, his first wife. But when his first marriage was ending and before he met Courtney, she told me they slept together a few times. It didn't last long, she said. Even if he hadn't met Courtney, it wasn't going anywhere, but once he met Courtney, that was definitely the end."

"She's lying," Violet said. The cookie she was holding in her hand snapped apart, scattering crumbs everywhere. "I saw them. Why would they be at Mario's together if they weren't having an affair? I saw them kiss!"

"She doesn't deny that," I said. "She explained that it was one of those weird coincidences. He had a business meeting cancel at the last minute, and she was having lunch with a friend, but the friend didn't show up. So, they had lunch together. They were friends, in a way, so it made sense. Dennis had ordered a bottle of wine already for his business lunch, and Tiffany ended up drinking too much and hugged and kissed him outside the restaurant. She claimed he pushed her away, but probably not before she got lipstick on his collar."

I paused. Violet's face was getting whiter and whiter. "You said you got back in your car and ducked down so they wouldn't catch you. Isn't in possible that you didn't see Dennis push her away?"

Violet shook her head, her face nearly frozen. "No," she whispered. "It's not possible. They were having an affair. *I saw it*. I saw it."

"My guess is you knew about Tiffany's herbal distributor from when Courtney worked there," I said cautiously. "She probably mentioned something to you. Since Tiffany has Jillian call her order in, I'm guessing Courtney called sometimes, too, and told you about it so that's how you knew. You may not have known specifically about Monkshood, but I bet you did know some herbs and flowers could be toxic. You were an avid gardener, after all. It wouldn't have been difficult to research. And it goes without saying that you would have known about the brandy and Dennis's cousin."

Violet sucked in her breath and turned away. "Who else knows?" she asked quietly, her voice defeated.

I crossed my fingers, praying I had made the right decision. "No one. For now. I was hoping you would come clean on your own. You don't want to let an innocent man go to jail for something you did."

"He's not innocent," she said. "He stole from people."

"And he'll be punished for stealing," I said. "But he shouldn't be punished for what he *didn't* do."

Violet was silent for a long time—so long, I was a little afraid she was going to tell me she didn't care. If she didn't confess, I had a feeling that would be the end. I suspected there would be no evidence against her ... nothing that couldn't also be used against Glenn.

"He wasn't supposed to die," she said finally, her voice cracking.

"What are you talking about? You put poison in his brandy."

"I put Monkshood in his brandy," she corrected.

"Which is a poison."

"At too high of a dose," she said. "At lower doses, it's used for pain relief. How else could I have bought it from an herb distributor?"

"That's true. It is used for pain relief. Is that what you were trying to do? Give Dennis something for pain? Was Dennis suffering?"

She shook her head. "I wasn't trying to use it medicinally. I wanted to make him sick."

"But not die."

"No."

"I don't understand."

She sighed, a long one, full of despair. She looked like she had aged about ten years since she'd answered the door. "My only daughter was about to give birth to my first grandchild, and she was in the pit of despair. She was sure her husband had fallen out of love with her, and nothing she was doing was changing that. She had convinced herself that once the baby was a little older and could be left with someone so she could go back to work, he would leave her.

"I begged her to sit down and have a heart-to-heart with Dennis, but she refused. She was sure that would just give him the opening he needed to ask her for a divorce. She thought the only thing saving her was that he didn't want to tell her while she was pregnant.

"I had to do something. The last thing I wanted was to see my daughter go through the struggles I went through when my husband walked out. Courtney was old enough to not require a sitter, so at least I didn't have to worry about that expense. But to watch her go through that heartache with a baby? I couldn't do it.

"For weeks, I racked my brain, trying to figure out how to make Dennis fall in love with her again. Then one night, I was flipping around the channels, and there was one of those made-for-TV movies on, where the husband is sick and ends up falling in love with the live-in nurse. And that's when it hit me. What if Dennis got sick ... really sick? Courtney of course would drop everything to nurse him back to health. And while she did that, she could make him fall in love with her again.

"It seemed perfect. Not only would Dennis be home, under Courtney's loving care, but he also wouldn't be seeing Tiffany at all. Out of sight, out of mind. It seemed like the answer to my prayers."

"If that's the case, why didn't you just slip something into a drink while you were there one night?" I asked. "Or, if you didn't want to be there, into one of the open bottles of brandy in his office?"

"Timing," she said. "I didn't want him to get sick after the baby was born. She couldn't play nurse to him then, because she would have the baby to worry about. Someone else would have to be in the house to help her, and even if that were me, I didn't want anything to get in the way of them falling in love again. All they were doing in December was going to parties. Party after party. There was no quiet evening when I could be sure he would drink the Monkshood.

"Giving it to him as a present seemed like the best option. I figured he would have a drink shortly after he opened the gift. And once he got sick, I could make sure no one else had any by 'accidentally' knocking the bottle over. And if it came up later, we could just chalk it up to a bad batch of brandy. It happens. But, instead, he drank too much and died before Courtney could get him to the hospital."

I chewed on my lip as I studied her. Was it possible? I didn't know how much Monkshood was in the bottle, but Wyle made it seem like there was quite a bit, and it didn't take much to be toxic. Was it really an innocent accident, as she said? That her intention really was just to make him sick, and she didn't realize she put in too much?

But then I remembered how she bought the Monkshood. Using Tiffany's account. Would someone who was only attempting to make someone sick cover her tracks so well?

Or, did she know exactly what she was doing all along?

"Why didn't you tell the police immediately after it happened?" I asked. "Why did you go through the whole charade of hiring me and having me look into it?"

She snapped her face around to look at me. "Because someone needed to look into Tiffany and Glenn," she cried. "They were guilty."

"Not of murder."

"No. But I knew something was wrong. That whole Maple Leaf Grove mess. Something was fishy with it. And Tiffany, well ..." her voice trailed off as if the sudden burst of anger had simply fizzled out.

"You really need to tell the police," I said quietly. "And Courtney, as well."

She sighed again, her skin grey. "I know," she said quietly. "I actually didn't think I would get away with it. I was shocked when they arrested Glenn. I told myself he deserved it. He was an awful boss, you know. I know I said before he was fine, but that wasn't the whole truth. Dennis was always nice to me, but Glenn treated everyone who worked for him like they were beneath him. It was nice to see him arrested, knowing he was getting a taste of his own medicine."

While I believed that Glenn was an awful boss, I wasn't sure I believed she would have eventually turned herself in.

"You're doing the right thing," I said.

She glanced at me, her eyes so much like Courtney's, it made my throat tighten. Courtney was about to give birth, and now, she'd have to navigate motherhood without her husband *or* her mother.

Violet gave me a sad smile. "I hope you're right."

Chapter 19

I stepped up onto the stoop, sucked in a deep breath of the frosty cold air, and rang the doorbell.

I had no idea how Courtney would react to seeing me. Because of me, she had lost her mother. Her husband was gone, too, and now, she was going to be truly alone with her new baby.

I listened to the soft footfalls as someone approached the door. Then, there was a long pause. I wondered if she was debating whether or not to open the door to me. Would it make sense to knock again, or just leave? As I considered my options, I heard the click of the deadbolt being pulled back, and the door opened.

I wasn't sure what I expected—her face red and puffy with tears again? Instead, it was composed and expressionless.

"Charlie," she said, her voice flat. "I wasn't expecting you."

I tried to smile as I held up a covered pan. "I hope it's not a bad time. I brought you some lasagna and tea."

She stared at me, her eyes as empty as glass, before turning around and walking away. For a moment, I could only stare at her retreating back, wondering what I should do, but as she left the door wide open, I took it as an invitation to enter. I stepped inside, closing the door behind me and pulling off my coat.

I found her in the kitchen, sitting at the table, a cup of tea in front of her. She didn't look at me as I put the lasagna in the fridge and the tea on the counter, nor did she offer me any sort of refreshment.

"I suppose I should thank you," she said, her voice hollow.

Cautiously I walked over to the table and slid into the seat across from her. "I'm not here for that."

"But still," she said. "You did get to the bottom of what happened. And now I know the truth."

Now that I was closer, I saw that I was wrong in thinking her face was expressionless. It was more like she was numb ... so shell-shocked from everything that had happened to her in the past few weeks that she had completely shut down emotionally.

"I'm sorry it was your mother."

She shrugged. "So am I."

I chewed on my lip. "Do you know what's happening with her?"

"It looks like there will be some sort of plea deal," she said. "I guess the prosecution doesn't want to throw the book at a soon-to-be-grandma who was only trying to help her daughter rekindle her marriage."

So, it appeared Violet had found a good enough lawyer to have convinced the legal system it was all a mistake. I wondered how the lawyer explained away using Tiffany's account. Or, maybe they decided Violet wasn't much of a public risk and wanted to just move on.

"That's good," I said. "Hopefully, she won't get as much jail time."

Courtney shrugged. "Maybe. Although I'm not sure how much I want to see her."

I blinked in surprise. "You don't want to see her?"

Courtney raised her face, fixing those strange, unsettling eyes on mine. "She killed my husband. The father of my baby."

"She was trying to help."

"She told me he was having an affair."

"She was mistaken," I said, wondering how I had found myself in a situation where I was defending Violet. "And, to be fair, what she saw was easy to misinterpret."

"That 'mistake' means my child will grow up without a father."

I couldn't argue with that.

"This is all my fault," Courtney said quietly.

I did a double take, wondering if I heard her correctly. "Wait. How is this *your* fault? You didn't poison anyone."

Her mouth was twisted. "I should have talked to Dennis," she said. "You were right. That's what most people would have done. Just asked their husband if they were having an affair. But not me. I bury my head in the sand, and look what happened. If I had had been braver, if I hadn't been so afraid he was going to leave me like my father left me, I could have told him what my mother saw. We could have talked about it … gotten to the bottom of it. Instead, I cheated on my husband and worked myself into such a state, my mother thought it was a good idea to poison my husband to bring us back together."

I was taken aback at the harshness in her tone. Her mouth pressed together so tightly, her lips had turned white. The numbness had slipped from her face like a mask, revealing the self-hatred beneath.

I took a deep breath, knowing I had to say something, but feeling like I had to tread very carefully. "While it's true you could have handled things better, this is still not your fault. Your mother is a grown-up who made her own decisions. Your husband made his own decisions. A marriage has two sides."

She stared at me, her face aghast. "You're blaming Dennis? He's dead!"

"This isn't about blame," I said. "It's about learning from your mistakes. It's about making better choices. And," I took another breath. "It's about forgiveness.'

She looked away. "I don't know if I can ever forgive my mother."

I let that slide. "What about yourself?"

Her face seemed to collapse on itself, like something inside her was cracking. "How can I? Dennis is dead. My mother is in jail. Look at the mess that's left."

"But that's what life is," I said. "It's messy. It's hard. It's uncomfortable. You're going to make mistakes. People around you are going to make mistakes. You're human. And if you don't learn to forgive, you're going to make life that much more difficult for yourself."

She was silent as she thought about what I said. "I don't know if I can."

"I didn't say you have to do it now," I said. "It takes time. And healing. And maybe you never will completely. But you can try. And that's what matters in the end."

She continued to sit there, pondering my words. Her face was thinner, I noticed. The skin stretched across her cheekbones. It made her look older.

Older and battle worn.

"Tiffany called me," she said, abruptly changing the subject.

I raised my eyebrows. "Really?"

Courtney nodded. "To apologize."

"Wow. That's a surprise."

Courtney's lips curled up in a tiny smile. "Yeah, it was a shock. But it was good. We had a good talk."

"Good," I said. I wondered if Courtney now knew the truth about Tiffany and Dennis, but I decided if she didn't bring it up, I didn't need to.

Courtney's smile became a little shy as she rubbed her belly. "She offered me my job back."

"Really?"

"Not right away, of course. I mean, it's more than just being pregnant. I need a little time. I forgive her, but … well. I need time. Besides, Tiffany said she has to build things back up. It's all a mess now, as you can imagine. But yeah." Her smile widened. "Even said I could bring the baby, and maybe we could offer childcare."

"Oh, that sounds like a smart idea."

"Yeah. She had talked about it before, offering something to make it easier for moms to work out, but she never was able to get it going. But, with my little one, maybe we can offer a whole new service."

"That's great news," I said. "I'm really happy for you. Maybe this will be the start of a whole new chapter for you."

Courtney nodded again, finally meeting my eyes. The hurt and grief were still there, but there was something else now, as well. Something that looked a little like hope. "Maybe," she agreed.

A Word From Michele

Hi there!

I hope you enjoyed *The Murder Before Christmas* as much as I enjoyed writing it. If you did, I would really appreciate it if you'd leave me a review and rating on Amazon or Goodreads.

If you want more Charlie, I've got you covered.

First off, you can access exclusive bonus scenes from *The Murder Before Christmas* for free right here:

MPWnovels.com/r/q/murder-before-christmas-bonus

In addition, if you keep reading, you can check out an excerpt from book 2, *Ice Cold Murder*, which is available here.

The *Charlie Kingsley Mysteries* series is actually a spin-off from my award-winning *Secrets of Redemption* series. *Secrets of Redemption* is a little different from the *Charlie Kingsley Mysteries,* as it's more psychological suspense, but it's still clean like a cozy.

You can learn more about both series, including how they fit together, at MPWNovels.com, along with lots of other fun things such as short stories, deleted scenes, giveaways, recipes, puzzles and more.

For now, turn the page for a sneak peek at *Ice Cold Murder.*

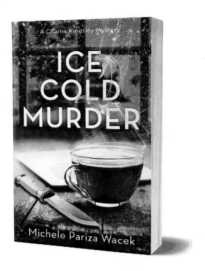

Ice Cold Murder - Chapter 1

"Are you out of your mind?" Pat's hand paused mid-air, chocolate chip cookie halfway to her mouth as she stared at me, eyes wide.

Forsaking her cookie like that, I knew she was serious.

"She asked," I said matter-of-factly. "I'm being a good friend."

"You're being insane," Pat muttered as her hand finally completed its journey. "Do you have any idea what you've agreed to?"

"Why yes," I said. "I agreed to accompany Claire to her grandmother's reading of the will."

"In a *haunted* house," Pat added.

I gave her a look. "Well, first off, as you know, *I* live in a haunted house. Why on Earth would spending the weekend at someone else's bother me?"

"And that leads me to the second issue," Pat said, waving the hand holding the cookie. Crumbs scattered everywhere, making me momentarily wish I had a dog instead of a cat. A dog would be on it already, cleaning up the mess. Midnight, my black cat, could care less. "Why would a reading of a will take an entire weekend?"

"Well, I grant you, that IS weird," I admitted.

"Did Claire have any explanation for it?"

"Not exactly."

Pat raised her eyebrows, clearly waiting for more.

I sighed. "I guess there are some ... issues, in the family."

Pat yelped. "Issues? You're willingly going to spend an entire weekend in a haunted house with a family working through their *issues*?"

I winced. When she put it like that, she definitely had a point. "So, to be fair, I didn't know about the haunted part until right now," I said. "Claire didn't mention that."

"But she mentioned the *issues*," Pat said. "And that didn't stop you from agreeing to this insanity?"

"It's hardly like that makes her family some sort of weird anomaly," I said, thinking of my own strained relationship with my sisters. "All families have issues. Which is part of why I decided to go. It's not *my* family, so I won't be triggered. It might be a little uncomfortable, but so what? I'm sure I'll survive. And Claire is worth it. If she needs a neutral, supportive person to help her though this, I'm happy to be that for her."

Pat gave me a look but kept her mouth shut. I was sure the same thoughts were running through her head that had gone through mine.

Ever since she had gotten pregnant with Daphne two-and-a-half years ago, Claire hadn't looked well. While I knew some of it was the result of grief—a couple of her good childhood friends had disappeared without a trace around the time she got pregnant—I had a feeling there was more to the story.

Something else was wrong with Claire. I wasn't entirely sure what, but my hope was that by accompanying her to this rather strange family obligation, she might trust me enough to share the truth of what was really going on with her.

"I don't know, Charlie," Pat said. "There's something about this that doesn't feel right."

Claire was the first person I met when I first arrived in Redemption, Wisconsin, completely by accident. The truth of the matter is that I was on the run from an abusive fiancé and only stopped in Redemption because I was lost. I never meant to stay, but as I've since learned, Redemption has its own ideas about who stays and who goes. Before I knew what was happening, I had bought a house (and not just any house, but what the locals considered the "most" haunted house in an already haunted town) and had opened a tea business out of it.

Pat was one of my first customers, and she also became one of my best friends … despite being well over a decade older than me. She was my "partner in crime," so to speak, as I found myself inadvertently roped into helping solve crimes related to my tea customers. Like everything else in Redemption, this was not anything I'd planned. I would have been quite happy to spend my days quietly puttering around in my garden and creating blends and tinctures. I very much disliked calling attention to myself, which unfortunately, solving crimes had a tendency to do.

But, alas, what I wanted had little to do with what I got.

At least this weekend trip, as uncomfortable as it might turn out, would provide me a reprieve from mystery-solving.

"I agree that it doesn't feel right," I said. "The fact that I'm going instead of Doug doesn't exactly help." Doug was Claire's husband and the father of her daughter.

"Speaking of which, why isn't Doug going?" Pat asked, selecting another cookie, even though I knew she'd end up complaining about the added calories ruining whatever current diet she was on. The best way to describe Pat was "round"— round face, round body, round black-rimmed glasses, and short, no-nonsense brown hair that was turning grey.

"Claire said because of Daphne. They don't have anyone who can take her with such short notice for three full days, and they think she's too young to come with them. Not to mention the house isn't exactly baby-proofed."

Pat rolled her eyes. "That's an understatement."

"It made sense when she explained it," I said. "The house is old, and I guess it hasn't been used a lot. Although Claire was rather vague about why."

"I'll tell you why," Pat said. "Because it's haunted. That's why."

I sighed. "All right. I'll bite. Tell me more."

"Well, I don't remember all the details," Pat said as I shook my head in exasperation. "Hey, it's Redemption," she said defensively. "I can't keep track of all the weird things that happen here. That'd be a full-time job."

"So, you don't have *all* the details, but I assume you have *some*?"

Pat glared at me. "You're *so* funny. Okay, this is what I know. About twenty or thirty years ago, or ..." she squished up her face. "Maybe it's longer. I can't remember anymore. Anyway, Florence, that's Claire's grandmother, decided to have some work done on the house. Was she redoing the kitchen? Maybe it was the basement. Anyway, whichever it was, something happened, and the contractor was killed."

My eyes widened. "Killed?"

Pat nodded. "Yeah, it was some freak accident. He fell off a ladder or something. Well, when they were investigating, it came out that there had been all sorts of weird stuff happening. Things kept getting moved around, even though everyone at the site swore they hadn't touched anything. Tools stopped working, and batteries would die, even if they were fresh. His assistant flat out refused to go back after his boss was killed. Said it was too creepy, and he didn't want anything to do with it."

"Wow," I said. "Was the work ever finished?"

Pat frowned. "I'm not sure. I do know it wasn't easy. A lot of contractors refused the project, and the few who took it ended up walking off the job."

"What did Florence say? She was living there when all this was happening, right?"

Pat shook her head. "No, it was always a second home. I'm not sure how Flo ended up with the house. If I recall, her husband's family bought it, and somehow, she ended up with it. But she always lived in town. She loved spending long weekends out there, though, even in the winter. She was big into cross-country skiing and ice skating. She just thought it was too remote to live there full time."

"Did she still go out there even after everything happened?"

"For a while, yes," Pat said. "Flo used to laugh about it. The ghosts, I mean. Said it was nothing compared to Helen's ... well, your house, now."

"So she didn't believe."

Pat hesitated. "Nooo. Not then, anyway. Although I think it did cause a rift in the family, as Claire's mom, Daisy, did believe in ghosts. I don't remember all the details now. It wasn't until Billy disappeared that everything changed."

"Who's Billy?"

"Flo's only son. Claire's uncle. I think it was, well, it has to be twenty years or so by now, which is why I think the contracting work was done earlier. Anyway, he disappeared, and Flo was so devastated, she quit nearly everything. Stopped going to church, stopped seeing friends, quit going up to the 'cottage,' as she called it, even though it's apparently huge. Bigger than most houses, anyway. So now do you see why this is all very peculiar? Her having the will reading in a house she probably hadn't even been to in twenty years?"

Now that Pat had explained the whole story, I was starting to understand her reaction to my going with Claire. "Did you know Flo?"

Pat nodded, her eyes sad. "I knew her through church. She was one of my Sunday School teachers, and later on, we served on some of the same volunteer committees. It wasn't like we were best friends or anything, but I liked her. Every time she was involved in something, it was always more fun." Pat picked up a napkin to dab her eyes. "I'm sorry she's gone, and I'm especially sorry that she never recovered from Billy's disappearance."

"What happened with Billy?"

Pat frowned. "It's been so long now. I seem to recall there was some sort of family fight. Billy was upset with someone else … Daisy, maybe?"

I gave her a surprised look. "Claire's mom?"

"Yeah, there was some conflict between Daisy and the rest of the family. Claire, too. I'm not sure about the details."

"What do you mean, 'Claire, too'?"

Pat sighed. "Again, Flo was always vague on specifics. The only thing that was clear was both Daisy and Claire are, well, I guess 'estranged' from the rest of the family. Although that's not quite the right word either, as I think they occasionally attend the big family get-togethers."

"Claire doesn't get along with the rest of her family?" This was news to me.

Pat gave me a look that clearly said, "Now do you get it?"

"It started with Daisy. Flo never really talked about it, but it was obvious Daisy was the black sheep. Then, when Claire and Amelia came along, Claire took on the same black-sheep role as her mom."

"Amelia?"

"Claire's sister."

"Claire has a sister?" More news.

Pat sat back in her chair with an "I told you so" smile, shaking her head. "Still think it's a good idea to go?"

"I think it's a little late to back out now."

When I first arrived in Redemption, lost and confused, I had decided to take a break and have a cup of coffee and bite to eat at Aunt May's Diner. I hoped it would clear my head and help me figure out how to get back to the main highway. Claire was my waitress. One thing led to another, and eventually, she became one of my best friends.

Which is why I found her not telling me about her sister peculiar. While I had never assumed she had shared *all* her secrets with me, having a sibling seemed like a pretty big life detail to have never mentioned.

Pat shrugged. "Your funeral. Hopefully, not literally."

I rolled my eyes. "Hopefully. Although I will say, this does shed a new light on the 'family issues.' A sister she doesn't talk about and the fact she and her mother are the black sheep of the family ... I wonder why she doesn't just go with her mother, then, instead of asking me."

Pat shifted in her seat as she reached for her tea. "I take it you also don't know that Daisy has dementia."

I pressed my hand against my lips. "Oh no."

Pat nodded sadly. "Yes, the whole situation is tragic. She's in a nursing home."

Again, I wondered how well I knew my friend. "When did this happen?"

"Oh, it's been years," Pat said. "A decade at least. Maybe longer. Long before you arrived. It was early onset, very early. I remember when it happened. Flo was beside herself with grief. First Billy disappeared, and then Daisy's health ... Flo was starting to feel like the family was cursed. Anyway, Claire never did like talking about it, so I'm not that surprised she never told you."

"Wow," I said, trying to take in everything Pat had shared. All that tragedy in one family. A haunted house. And a will reading on top of it all. No wonder Pat thought I was crazy.

For a moment, I toyed with the idea of backing out, but even as the thought entered my mind, I dismissed it. Claire needed me. The tone of desperation when she asked me to go made that clear. I didn't understand it at the time ... thought maybe I'd mistaken grief for desperation. But now, I knew that wasn't the case.

She needed me to be with her. Not Doug, her husband, but me.

And I couldn't let her down.

"Still going?" Pat asked me, raising an eyebrow.

"I think it would be really crappy of me to back out now," I said. "Plus, it's only a weekend. I can survive a weekend."

Pat let out a guffaw.

"You'll still keep an eye on Midnight, right?"

Upon hearing his name, Midnight opened one green eye and looked at me. He was curled up on the seat of one of the kitchen chairs, which of course was pushed close to the window, so he could bask in the sunlight.

Pat shifted her gaze over to the cat. "Of course. A poor, innocent animal shouldn't have to suffer for his human's mistakes."

Midnight closed his eye and presumably went back to sleep.

"Clearly, he appreciates you feeling his pain," I said.

Ice Cold Murder - Chapter 2

"So, you want to tell me a little bit more about this will reading?"

Claire barely glanced at me as she carefully maneuvered her car through town on the surprisingly busy streets. Snow was falling—not heavily enough to impact visibility, but the road was getting slippery. "What do you want to know?" Under her cheery, red, knitted cap, her face was pale, and there were tension lines at the corners of her hazel eyes.

"Well, it's kind of strange, isn't it? A will reading taking place over a weekend in a remote cottage? It feels more like a family holiday than something that typically only takes an hour in a lawyer's office."

A small smile touched Claire's lips. "That's my Grandma Flo for you. She always had to be different." The smile faded, and she let out a sigh. "I know there are things I should have told you sooner. It's not that I don't want you to know. It's just difficult to talk about. But isn't family stuff always that way?" She threw me a sideways glance. "What did Pat tell you?"

"How do you know Pat told me anything?"

She gave me a look. "Oh, come now. You really think I don't know you told Pat?"

"Well, I did ask her to watch Midnight."

"Of course you did."

"I wasn't trying to gossip behind your back or anything," I started to say, but she waved a hand at me.

"I know. That's not what I meant to imply. I know you would never intentionally hurt me. Why do you think I asked you to come? All that said, I also know Pat."

"She wasn't trying to hurt you, either," I said, feeling a need to defend my friend.

Claire looked at me, bemused. "I'm sure she wasn't. I just know how much she likes, ah, 'sharing' stories about her fellow friends and neighbors."

"Well." I couldn't think of anything to say, as Claire was right. Pat did love to gossip. "She did warn me ... said I was going to be staying in a haunted house."

I half-expected Claire to laugh, but instead, her nose wrinkled in concentration. "I don't know if the house is 'haunted,' per se. Not like your house. But there *is* something there." She shivered, and then paused to carefully turn down one of the main roads that headed out of town.

I gave her a questioning look. "What do you mean, 'something's there'?"

"It's hard to explain. Initially, it seemed fine. Growing up, I visited the house regularly, and when I think back to my childhood, most of my memories are happy." She hesitated and narrowed her eyes as she gripped the steering wheel harder.

"'Most'?"

She pursed her lips. "You know those days that start out sunny and beautiful, but then suddenly in the afternoon, a rainstorm appears out of nowhere? All of the sudden, it's dark and cloudy and cold, and maybe there's even thunder and lightning. And, then, the storm blows through, the clouds part, and it's sunny again. That house is like that. There are these moments when everything just seems ... dark. Like a shadow falls over the whole place. It's dark and heavy, and hard to move ... it's even hard to breathe. In fact, I remember when a friend of mine went up with me one year. She had asthma, and when that shadow fell over everything, it caused a terrible asthma attack. It was so bad, we ended up taking her to the hospital. Needless to say, that was the end of our friendship. But, anyway, back to these ... well, 'dark spells,' I guess ... just as quickly as they appear, they disappear. Just like that, everything clears up, and it's all back to the way it was. It leaves you wondering if you imagined the darkness altogether. But you know in your heart, you didn't."

I could feel my chest tightening up just listening to her. Maybe Pat was right, and this was a mistake. "Was it during one of these 'dark spells' that the contractor died?"

Claire pressed her lips together. "Probably. I wasn't there, of course, so I can't be sure. But if I had to guess, yes."

"So, what's the story with that?"

The snow was starting to come down more heavily. Claire squinted at the windshield and eased her foot off the gas. "Over the years, Grandma had been hiring workers and whatnot to do small remodeling projects. She always scheduled them for while she was there, so she could keep an eye on things, she said. But I think it was because of the dark spells. She wanted to be there so in case one of them happened, she could smooth things out."

"So your family knew about the dark spells?"

Claire's mouth twisted in a sideways smile. "That's a loaded question."

"What do you mean?"

"Of course they did. How could they not? But what they choose to acknowledge now is something else altogether."

"I don't understand."

Claire glanced at me, her eyes haunted. "You will. But to answer your question about Grandma, yes, she knew about the dark spells. Yet if you asked her about them, she would say it was all nonsense. Just like the house being haunted was nonsense. She didn't believe in ghosts, and felt there was nothing wrong with the house.

"Be that as it may, she always made sure she was there when the house was being worked on, and she kept the projects small enough so she could work them around her schedule. But then she decided she wanted to completely remodel the basement—turn it into a massive den with a game room and bar. It was to give us kids more indoor activity options when the weather was bad outside. Especially in the winter, there were days it was too cold to be outside for long.

"This project was too big for her to be there all the time. And, of course, when the contractor died, she wasn't there."

"Do you know how he died?"

She shook her head. "Some freak accident. I can't quite re-member. But I do know that the other contractor who was with him completely flipped out. He was convinced the house *was* haunted, and by something dangerous. Not surprisingly, he re-fused to finish the job. Also not surprisingly, other contractors heard about it and didn't want anything to do with the house, either. The few who were brave, or desperate, enough for the work didn't last long. I don't think anything necessarily hap-pened to them; the house was just completely tainted. Needless to say, the basement was never finished."

"What about you? Did you still spend time in the house after the contractor died?"

"At first, yes. My grandmother didn't want to admit that anything was wrong. She was trying to prove a point. So she made us all go up like everything was just fine. But," Claire paused, biting her lip. "There WAS something wrong. Some-thing changed after the contractor died. It's hard to explain, but everything just felt … different. Maybe it was because we were all uneasy, knowing someone had died there just a few months earlier. Or, maybe the house was haunted. Either way, no one seemed to be having all that much fun there anymore. Even my grandmother was uncomfortable. So, over time, our visits just started petering out.

"My mother especially never wanted to go. She was always anxious there. But before the contractor died, she seemed more willing to deal with it. I think she wanted to keep the peace with the family, so she basically closed her mouth and did what she had to. But after the contractor died, I think it was all too much. She just couldn't handle being there anymore. I was glad we stopped the visits. I didn't like it, either. When I was young, it was fine, but the older I got, the more uneasy I felt there, too. Still, my grandmother never wanted to hear anything against it. She used to claim we were all just trying to cause trouble." Even though her expression didn't change, there was a tension in Claire's body that hadn't been there earlier.

"Why would your grandmother have such a reaction?"

Claire shook her head. "I'm not sure. Something happened when my mother was a child, but she would never talk about it. Said it wasn't anything a child needed to deal with. But once I got old enough to have that conversation, she was diagnosed with dementia. So, that was kind of that."

"I'm sorry to hear about your mother," I said.

Claire nodded tightly. "I should have told you sooner," she said again. "Just like I should have told you about my sister. Did Pat say anything?"

"She did. But all I know is that you *have* a sister. Nothing else."

"Did she tell you about my mother?"

"Yes. But, again, no specifics. Just that she's in a nursing home."

"Well, that's pretty much the whole story," Claire said. "She went downhill quickly. Physically, she's in good shape, but mentally, she's pretty far gone. Occasionally, she still has moments of lucidity, but they've been getting fewer and further between over the years."

I reached over to put a hand on her knee. "I really am sorry."

Claire glanced at me and smiled slightly, a sheen to her eyes. "Thanks. So, what else did Pat say?"

I took my hand off her knee and leaned back in my seat. "That there was a rift between you and your mother and the rest of the family. But again, she didn't know why."

Claire went back to focusing on her driving. "That's a nice way of saying it."

"Is that why you didn't tell me about your sister? Or anything about your family?"

Claire frowned as she thought about it. "I guess 'yes' would be the easy answer, but it's more complicated than that," she said finally. "It's more because I don't want to think about it. I don't like talking about it, because then I have to think about it, and it's not something I want to think about. I can't do anything about it now." She glanced sideways at me again. "I don't want you to take this the wrong way, because we would have been friends regardless, but I really loved the fact that you didn't know my history. Everyone else here does, so I could never escape it. But you were always so relaxing to be around, because I knew I never had to talk about it."

"I get it," I said, thinking about my own history I had escaped from. Coming to Redemption meant I didn't have to talk about what I had left in New York. "It's not like I want to talk about my past, either."

She smiled slightly. "That's for sure. You're the worst." Her smile faded. "But seriously, it's been painful. My mother was my best friend and biggest champion. When she was diagnosed with dementia, it was like the bottom dropped out of my world. I didn't feel like I had a family anymore."

"I get it," I said, and I did. No one in my family understood why I had just upped and left New York and moved out to a small town in Wisconsin. None of them had believed my fiancé was abusive—they all thought I was exaggerating. Worse, they still hadn't completely forgiven me.

"I know you do." The look in her eyes reflected the pain that was probably mirrored in mine.

"So, what happened? Why the family rift?"

She blew the air out her cheeks with a loud noise. "You know how I sometimes just know things?" She paused, eyeing me nervously, as if I might suddenly jump out of the car rather than listen to what she had to say. "Or how I get feelings about things, even though they haven't happened yet?"

I nodded.

"Well, my mother did, as well. Hers were stronger than mine, though. Anyway, we're the only two. The rest of the family doesn't have anything like that, according to them."

I waited as Claire slowed down to turn on an even narrower country road. The snow was starting to accumulate faster, leaving small mounds on the side of the road. "And ..." I prompted when she didn't say anything.

"And, what?"

"What else? There has to be more."

Claire sighed. "There probably is, but I don't know it. All I know is my grandmother hated any talk about either my mother or I feeling or knowing anything. That's one of the reasons she never wanted to hear anything about anything being off with the cottage. I don't know the history or what happened when my mom was a child, but whatever it was, neither my grandmother nor my Aunt Iris wanted to hear a word about any kind of 'knowing' or 'feeling' my mother or I had. It actually wasn't until I was older that it started happening to me. But when it did, it drove a wedge between me and the rest of family. Especially Amelia."

"Your sister?"

She nodded. "We were close when we were kids. But as we grew older and I started having the same experiences as my mother, Amelia stopped wanting to have anything to do with me. She started hanging around my Aunt Iris and our cousins more than me." She let go of the steering wheel to swipe at her eyes, but not before I saw the pain reflected there.

"That's rough," I said.

"Yeah. It was. It was right around the time my Uncle Billy disappeared, too, which made things even more difficult." She shot me a look. "I'm sure Pat told you about that?"

"Yeah, she did mention you had an uncle who disappeared."

Claire nodded. "When that happened, it was the final straw. No one went to the cabin after that. Not even my grandma. Well, other than a handful of visits a year just to check on things. One of the neighbors used to stop by regularly, as well. If I remember correctly, he also used to do small repairs and other handyman-type work up there. But that was it."

"If no one was using the cabin anymore, why didn't she sell it?"

Claire snorted. "Think selling a haunted cabin is easy? Try selling your house, and see what happens."

She had a point. "She could have sold it to someone outside the area, though. To someone who hadn't heard the stories about it being haunted."

"Yes, but when that person saw the basement half-finished and asked what happened, the realtor would have to disclose the contractor's death, and that they were never able to find someone to finish. As you can imagine, that pretty much ends the discussion."

"So your grandma has just hung onto it for all these years?"

"Pretty much."

"Wow." It was so peculiar to me. "I'm surprised she didn't try to do something about it. Did she ever think about asking the neighbor-handyman to finish the basement?"

"I'm not sure. But quite honestly, I don't know if she would have sold it, anyway."

"Why not?"

Claire frowned. "She had an … attachment, to the cottage. I guess that's the easiest way to explain it. She just loved it so, and even after everything that happened, she couldn't let go of it. And to be fair, there were a lot of good memories associated with the cabin, as well. So, she may have been holding onto hope that we could all eventually get back there again. Especially if Uncle Billy ever turned up."

"I guess that makes sense." I watched as Claire made another careful turn and began climbing deeper into the woods. "Boy, the snow is really coming down now." It was in fact blanketing the trees, weighing down their branches with mounds of white.

"Yeah, this time of year was always the most fun at the cabin." She smiled briefly. "I don't know that we'll be doing a lot of snow fort making and snowball fighting this time, though."

"What *do* you think we're going to be doing? I mean, this is a little crazy, having to spend a weekend up here, considering everything you've said. Don't you think?"

"It is, but it isn't. Like I said, grandma loved it so. I'm wondering if she was trying to get us to recapture the fun we used to have there. One last time, before it gets sold."

"You think it's going to sell now?"

"I don't see anyone in the family hanging on to it."

"But if a haunted house didn't sell years before, why would it now?"

"Because I think whoever inherits it will be motivated to sell," she said, "and willing to do whatever it takes to make that happen. If we have to finish the basement, the basement will get finished, one way or another. If we have to drop the price, we'll drop the price. At this point, I don't see anyone simply hanging on to it for old time's sake."

I studied Claire's determined face, the set of her mouth. "Do you think you'll inherit it?"

"I have no idea, but that's why I'm going," she said.

I gave her a surprised look. I never thought Claire to be so mercenary.

She saw my expression. "Not for me," she said. "For Daphne."

"You think your daughter might inherit it?"

"Daphne is her only great-granddaughter," she said. "Or great anything. Neither my sister nor cousins have any children yet. So, yeah, I think it's possible. And for my daughter's sake, I'll deal with whatever happens. But ..." she paused, and her face grew pensive. "I do want to say goodbye, as well. Grandma was thrilled when Daphne was born. She was so excited to be a great-grandma. Having Daphne gave me the opportunity to heal my relationship with her, which was just, well, wonderful." She gave me a faint smile. "It made me realize how much I missed having a relationship with my family. After my mom went into the nursing home, I pushed a lot of those feelings down. They were just too painful. But these past couple of years with grandma ... well, it was really nice."

"I'm glad you had that time with her," I said.

She nodded. "Thank you. I am, too. Oh, look, we're here." She made another tight turn onto a very narrow road. Actually, it was more like a path than a road. The tire tracks lining it made it clear we weren't the first to arrive. We continued on, the tires crunching over the packed snow as tree branches scratched the windshield.

"There's a larger parking area past the house," Claire said, driving very slowly. "Hopefully, it's been maintained. Grandma put it there so we would have room for all the cars during our getaways, and I suspect we'll need it today."

"How many people do you think will be here?"

Claire frowned. "Hard to say. Maybe a dozen?"

"*A dozen?*" Now that the reality of what I had agreed to was sinking in, the idea of spending a weekend in a small, remote cabin with a dozen people I didn't know was making me feel overwhelmed. "How big is the cabin? Where are we all going to sleep?" Outside, the snow fell harder, obscuring the view of the stark trees naked of leaves. Pat had warned me it was secluded, but I hadn't realized exactly how much so until that moment. I couldn't even remember the last time I had seen another house.

Claire grinned at me, the first true smile I had seen on her face in a long time. "Trust me, it won't be a problem. The cabin is huge. Five bedrooms plus a living room and den. The den also has a pullout couch. We'll bunk together in one of the rooms."

"They know I'm coming?"

"Well, they know I'm bringing a guest, yes. I didn't specify who."

I shot Claire a look. Great. Perfect start to this perfectly weird weekend. I wasn't even expected.

"There's the cabin," she said, pointing to her side of window as we continued to slowly drive by. I didn't get much sense of what it looked like other than the logs and sloping roof covered in mounds of snow.

"Looks like we will be able to park in the parking area. I can see cars."

I peered out of the windshield and spotted a black truck, blue SUV, and a couple mid-size cars already too covered in snow to make out the colors. Claire carefully pulled into a spot and turned off the engine.

"We made it."

Want to keep reading? Grab your copy of *Ice Cold Murder* here.

https://www.amazon.com/gp/product/B09L1JN8J3/

More *Charlie Kingsley Mysteries:*
A Grave Error (a free prequel novella)
Ice Cold Murder (Book 2)
Murder Next Door (Book 3)
Murder Among Friends (Book 4)
The Murder of Sleepy Hollow (Book 5)
Red Hot Murder (Book 6)
A Wedding to Murder For (novella)
Loch Ness Murder (novella)

Secrets of Redemption *series:*
It Began With a Lie (Book 1)
This Happened to Jessica (Book 2)
The Evil That Was Done (Book 3)
The Summoning (Book 4)
The Reckoning (Book 5)
The Girl Who Wasn't There (Book 6)
The Room at the Top of the Stairs (Book 7 coming soon)
The Secret Diary of Helen Blackstone (free novella)

Standalone books:
Today I'll See Her (free novella or purchase with bonus content)
The Taking
The Third Nanny
Mirror Image
The Stolen Twin

Access your free exclusive bonus scenes from *The Murder Before Christmas* right here:
MPWnovels.com/r/q/murder-before-christmas-bonus

Acknowledgements

It's a team effort to birth a book, and I'd like to take a moment to thank everyone who helped, especially my wonderful editor, Megan Yakovich, who is always so patient with me, Rea Carr for her expert proofing support, and my husband Paul, for his love and support during this sometimes-painful birthing process.

Any mistakes are mine and mine alone.

About Michele

A USA Today Bestselling, award-winning author, Michele taught herself to read at 3 years old because she wanted to write stories so badly. It took some time (and some detours) but she does spend much of her time writing stories now. Mystery stories, to be exact. They're clean and twisty, and range from psychological thrillers to cozies, with a dash of romance and supernatural thrown into the mix. If that wasn't enough, she posts lots of fun things on her blog, including short stories, puzzles, recipes and more, at MPWNovels.com.

Michele grew up in Wisconsin, (hence why all her books take place there), and still visits regularly, but she herself escaped the cold and now lives in the mountains of Prescott, Arizona with her husband and southern squirrel hunter Cassie.

When she's not writing, she's usually reading, hanging out with her dog, or watching the Food Network and imagining she's an awesome cook. (Spoiler alert, she's not. Luckily for the whole family, Mr. PW is in charge of the cooking.)

Made in United States
North Haven, CT
12 November 2022

26612068R00113